The guards were fully alert

This won't be easy, Katz thought as he examined the temple from between the leafy ferns.

He lay on his belly, his MP-5 subgun pressed against his side as he studied the layout of the area. Just ahead was an odd-looking fern, its leaves fanning out in a heart-shaped pattern. It somehow seemed out of place, and suddenly Katz realized what it was.

It was a detection device—the leaves plastic and the stem painted aluminum. If the surveillance system was sophisticated enough, it would register body temperature or heartbeats, and maybe even distinguish human intruders from other large mammals. At least one member of his assault force would surely trigger the detectors.

Bursts of automatic fire from a terrace confirmed Katz's fears. Orange flame streaked from the muzzles of assault rifles as the terrorists opened fire. Screams followed the volley of bullets, and Katz realized with a sinking feeling that they could have come from his men.

The enemy knew they had arrived, and the terrorists were chopping them down with automatic fire before Phoenix Force and their Indonesian allies could even get into position.

Mack Bolan's

PHOENIX FORCE.

#1 Argentine Deadline
#2 Guerilla Games
#3 Atlantic Scramble
#4 Tigers of Justice
#5 The Fury Bombs
#6 White Hell
#7 Dragon's Kill
#8 Aswan Hellbox
#9 Ultimate Terror
#10 Korean Killground
#11 Return to Armageddon
#12 The Black Alchemists
#13 Harvest Hell
#14 Phoenix in Flames
#15 The Viper Factor
#16 No Rules, No Referee
#17 Welcome to the Feast
#18 Night of the Thuggee
#19 Sea of Savages
#20 Tooth and Claw
#21 The Twisted Cross
#22 Time Bomb
#23 Chip Off the Bloc
#24 The Doomsday Syndrome
#25 Down Under Thunder
#26 Hostaged Vatican

#27 Weep, Moscow, Weep
#28 Slow Death
#29 The Nightmare Merchants
#30 The Bonn Blitz
#31 Terror in the Dark
#32 Fair Game
#33 Ninja Blood
#34 Power Gambit
#35 Kingston Carnage
#36 Belgrade Deception
#37 Show of Force
#38 Missile Menace
#39 Jungle Sweep
#40 Rim of Fire
#41 Amazon Strike
#42 China Command
#43 Gulf of Fire
#44 Main Offensive
#45 African Burn
#46 Iron Claymore
#47 Terror in Guyana
#48 Barracuda Run
#49 Salvador Assault
#50 Extreme Prejudice
#51 Savage World

PHOENIX FORCE.

GAR WILSON

SAVAGE WORLD

A GOLD EAGLE BOOK FROM

W✺RLDWIDE.

TORONTO • NEW YORK • LONDON • PARIS
AMSTERDAM • STOCKHOLM • HAMBURG
ATHENS • MILAN • TOKYO • SYDNEY

First edition January 1991

ISBN 0-373-61351-2

Special thanks and acknowledgment to
William Fieldhouse for his contribution to this work.

1

"Good morning, Mr. President," Hal Brognola said as he entered the Oval Office. "I won't ask how you are today. You wouldn't have called me to meet you if everything was just fine."

The President of the United States looked at Brognola and nodded. He was almost halfway through his first term in the White House and already looked as if he had aged five years, although in fact fewer than two had passed since he had been sworn in as commander-in-chief. Tons of pressure and responsibility come with the highest executive office in the land. Brognola knew all about pressure and responsibility himself.

"We need to talk," the President said as he stood up and came out from behind his desk to stand on the great gold seal of his office in the center of the carpet.

Brognola glanced toward the window behind the President's desk. The thick drapes were pulled across to blot out the familiar view of the Capitol Building and the Washington Monument in the distance. Brognola was not sure anyone could see through the glass from the outside. Maybe that was why the President had closed the drapes.

Security was vital to the existence of Brognola's organization. The President too would appreciate the importance of security, since he was formerly a director of the CIA...not that this was necessarily favorable, in Brognola's opinion. He was a veteran federal agent himself. Although Brognola had no official title and the outfit he commanded was not in any file, he was actually the highest-ranking Fed in the United States. He had dealt with government bureaucracy countless times in the past and knew it could screw up anything, including law enforcement and intelligence organizations.

The President preceded Brognola from the Oval Office and along a corridor to an elevator. He waved aside a couple of Secret Service agents. The pair glared at Brognola suspiciously, as if he were responsible for preventing them from doing their job. He was used to it, fully aware that they probably thought he might be a terrorist disguised in a baggy cheap suit that smelled of even cheaper cigars.

Brognola didn't present the polished, neat appearance associated with White House personnel, employees or visitors. He had a five-o'clock shadow at ten in the morning, and his necktie was loosened to leave the top button of his shirt open at the throat. The Fed presented a stark contrast to the dapper President as they stepped into the elevator.

Neither man spoke as the car descended to a section beneath the White House basement. Few people knew about this secret subterranean level beneath the commander-in-chief's office. Brognola had been to this covert area several times before. The President was reluctant to speak until they were safely below ground and surrounded by concrete and steel.

"The country needs your services again, Mr. Brognola," the President announced as they emerged into a narrow corridor. "But that must be obvious."

"Nothing is really obvious in my business," the Fed replied. "I never know for sure when you call me in if you have another assignment or you've decided to give me the sack."

"Unfortunately," the President said grimly, "I don't think the world is going to improve to such a degree that we won't need you or Stony Man operations."

Fluorescent lights from the ceiling illuminated their path as they walked to a room at the end of the hall. The President unlocked the door and escorted Brognola inside. The underground apartment was completely equipped with kitchen, bathroom, bedrooms, sofa, bookcases, TV and VCR. It had its own air supply, which began to pump in through wall vents the moment the elevator began to descend the shaft.

The secret quarters were an emergency shelter for the President in case of an attack on the White House. It wouldn't hold up well under a nuclear strike, but it would be ideal for surviving a conventional assault by terrorists or would-be revolutionaries armed with anything short of ballistic missiles. Brognola was not sure when the shelter had been constructed. Some time between the Kennedy assassination and the end of the Reagan Administration, he reckoned.

"Did you tell your people I was impressed by the way they handled that sensitive mission last month?" the President inquired as he closed and locked the door.

"Yeah," Brognola replied. "They're pretty impressive most of the time. So what do you have for us this time, Mr. President? Some work in the Middle East?"

"Why do you think it would be the Middle East?" the commander-in-chief asked with a slight smile as he moved to the kitchen and removed two glasses from a cabinet.

"Things are always bad there and they're getting worse," the Fed answered. "My guys were chomping at the bit to move against the terrorist kidnappers in Lebanon after they saw that videotape of Colonel Higgins hanging from the rafters with a rope around his neck. They wanted to go with or without your permission.''

The President poured bottled water into each glass as he spoke. ''There are reasons why we didn't want your people involved in that case. Political reasons that I don't imagine you'd have much sympathy for.''

''I guess my sympathy goes to Colonel Higgins and his family and the families of the other hostages still held in Lebanon,'' Brognola said with a shrug. ''Not a hell of a lot left over to feel much for 'political reasons' as to why we aren't doing more about the situation.''

''You're not afraid to speak your mind, Mr. Brognola,'' the President remarked. His tone suggested he didn't really appreciate the Fed's honesty. ''Glass of water?''

''Thank you,'' Brognola replied as he accepted the glass. ''Well, I guessed wrong about the Middle East. Where's the newest hot spot this time?''

''What do you know about Indonesia?'' the President asked as he unlocked the drawer of a filing cabinet.

''Indonesia? Not much, I guess. Not sure I could even find it on the map without hunting for a while. Of course, I wasn't aware there were any major risks to American interests in Indonesia since the 1960s, when Washington was afraid the country might swing over to communism.''

''Well, America still has a strong interest in Indonesia,'' the President declared. ''American oil companies, commodities exchange, mining corporations and our intelligence networks are all involved there.''

He removed a file folder from the cabinet and sat at the kitchen table and opened it. Brognola took the seat beside him.

"Here it is," the commander-in-chief announced, extracting a computer printout sheet in the folder. "There have been a number of violent demonstrations against the Golkar Party and the Indonesian president. That's not terribly unusual. However, they have also been strongly anti-American, and they accuse the United States of controlling the Indonesian government. Needless to say, that means the U.S. is also being blamed for all the social ills and shortcomings of Indonesia."

"What sort of shortcomings?" Brognola asked with a frown.

"The sort that has attracted the attention of Amnesty International and other human rights organizations over the years," the President answered. "It's hard to say how much of this criticism is deserved, but Secretary of State George Shultz thought the violations in 1984 were more serious. Supposedly more than a hundred thousand people in East Timor were either killed or died of starvation and disease."

"It's always nice when the United States of America is associated with that sort of behavior," the Fed muttered. "So there are anti-American demonstrations going on all over the world...including in the U.S. Remember that anarchist convention in Berkeley in July, 1989?"

"I'd like to forget about that," the President admitted. "But worse things are happening in Indonesia than riots and flag burning. Two American photographers made a trip to the mangroves of Borneo three days ago. They never returned. However, a package arrived at the U.S. Embassy in Djakarta just a few hours ago."

He handed a Telecopy of a photograph to Brognola. The grainy reproduction was clear enough to reveal the photo had been taken in an office. A large cardboard box sat on a floor beside a desk. Two melon-shaped objects were inside the box, but melons do not have hair, eyes or noses.

"Jesus," Brognola rasped. "I take it these are the heads of the missing wildlife photographers?"

"Except they weren't wildlife photographers. That was their cover while they were actually scouting a new site in Borneo for a listening station," the President explained.

"So they were CIA?" the Fed asked.

"NSA," the President replied. "The Telecopy and the enclosed report were delivered to National Security Agency headquarters here in Washington. One problem we have is there's no way of knowing if the two agents were killed because they were Americans or because someone knew they were NSA."

"They could have been killed simply because they were in the wrong place at the wrong time," Brognola remarked. "I don't know much about Borneo, but I understand it has some pretty untamed regions."

"I doubt tribal headhunters would send their trophies to the U.S. Embassy," the commander-in-chief remarked.

"They might if it was supposed to be a warning for others with U.S. passports to keep out of their territory," Brognola suggested. "We have to consider all the possibilities, although I agree that one seems least likely."

"Our NSA personnel in Indonesia may be burned," the President stated. "Their security could be ruined. For all we know, the enemy knows who they are and what they've been doing. We must assume the same may be true about CIA operations there, as well."

"So you want Stony Man to handle it because my people don't belong to either organization," Brognola guessed.

"Even I don't know who they are," the President said as he sipped some water. "I only know them by their code names. This is the sort of mission Phoenix Force is equipped to handle.''

"I'm not so sure about that," Brognola replied. "This sounds more like an intelligence investigation. Phoenix Force is used for direct action, not Intelligence gathering."

"They've handled numerous missions that required locating their opponents first," the President stated. "Phoenix Force has a one hundred percent success rate. You've told me that yourself."

"Yeah," the Fed growled. "Sometimes I have a big mouth. This is gonna be tough, Mr. President. My guys won't be able to work with NSA or CIA. That would pretty much defeat the purpose of using them. I'm not sure how to go about this one."

"Of course it's tough." The President smiled dryly. "That's why I'm giving it to you, Mr. Brognola."

"Thanks," Brognola said. "We'll try not to disappoint you."

"You never have before," the President reminded him.

2

"It's been a while since our paths crossed," Mack Bolan commented as he rose from a seat at the conference table. "Good to see you again."

"My pleasure," Yakov Katzenelenbogen replied with a gentle smile. "A rather rare pleasure since we always seem to be missing each other with various assignments in the field."

Bolan shook Katz's extended left hand firmly. The Israeli did not offer his right hand because he did not have one. His right arm had been amputated at the elbow long ago. Now he wore a prosthesis attached to the stump. Most people were uncomfortable shaking hands with the steel hooks at the end of an artificial limb.

Not that it would bother Bolan. The veteran of a thousand battlefields wasn't upset by such "physical imperfections." Katz had extraordinary courage, strong principles and he was totally dedicated to the good fight. It was the same fight that Bolan had been part of since he'd first committed himself to a one-man war against the Mafia. He had brought the deadly combat skills he'd learned in Vietnam to the big-city jungles where the man-beasts of organized crime prey on society.

As the Executioner, Bolan had chopped down syndicate killers, drug kingpins and mafioso crime lords. His odds had been a million to one against his surival, but Bolan had beaten them and the grim reaper. However, Bolan's war had not ended there. He was chosen to found the Stony Man operations. Together with Hal Brognola, Mack Bolan had created the supersecret organization to combat the growing menace of international terrorism. They had also assembled two special fighting units.

Able Team had been comprised of fellow veterans of Bolan's war against the Mafia. The men for the second unit, Phoenix Force, had been selected from the best operatives in the fields of espionage, antiterrorist squads and elite military outfits of the free world. Five very special men were chosen for the ranks of Phoenix. Yakov Katzenelenbogen was the ideal choice for unit commander of the remarkable commando team.

Mack Bolan rarely met a man with more battlefield experience than his own, but Katz was such a man. Indeed, the Israeli's career as a warrior, espionage agent and antiterrorist had started before Bolan was even born. Katz had fought the Nazis as a teenager in Europe. After World War II he had moved to Palestine to join the struggle for independence of the Jewish State of Israel. He had lost his right arm during a desert battle in the Six Day War, but continued to serve in the Israeli military and later in the Mossad intelligence network.

Middle-aged, slighty overweight, with clipped iron-gray hair and a kindly face, Katzenelenbogen seemed an unlikely candidate for a super commando or a master spy. Yet Katz was all that and much more. Bolan and the Israeli warhorse were genuinely glad to see one another. They respected and admired each other as men of courage and dedication who rarely meet their peers.

"I'm afraid we don't have time to chat," Bolan said with a sigh. "I'm on my way out. Got another mission."

"Yes," Katz remarked with a nod. "Needless to say, that's why I'm here, too."

He glanced around the War Room. The chairs around the conference table were empty. Blinking colored lights flashed on a massive map of the world that covered most of one wall. A yellow light meant that a situation in that part of the world threatened to become critical. A red light meant it already was critical, and a blue light indicated that the main cause of a problem was neutralized and the local authorities were in the process of mopping up what was left. Katz couldn't recall looking at the map without finding at least two blinking red lights.

"Hal is checking with the Bear about some computer data concerning another mission," Bolan explained. He guessed that Katz was wondering where the Fed was. "That's probably yours, Yakov."

"Lucky me," Katz replied as he removed a newspaper from under his right armpit and tossed it on the table.

Bolan glanced down at the paper. *Corriere della Sera* was printed across the logo on the front page.

"The *Evening Courier*," he read. "That's one of the most widely read newspapers in Rome and Milan, as I recall."

"That's right," Katz replied. "I didn't know you read Italian."

"I picked up a little over the years," Bolan answered with a slight grin. "I remember reading your file when you first came to Stony Man, Yakov. It had you listed as a master linguist, fluent in six languages, but Italian wasn't one of them."

"Well, I've been trying to improve my vocabulary in it for the last three or four years," Katz explained. "I've also been trying to enhance my grasp of some other languages."

"I'd think keeping up with six languages would be hard enough," Bolan said admiringly.

"My father was fluent in eighteen languages."

"Eighteen?" Bolan asked with surprise. "That's astonishing."

"Well, he was a translator and scholar of languages," Katz explained. "He didn't spend most of his time carrying out commando missions or training with small arms and martial arts. He was a superb linguist. He had quite a reputation in Russia, but he moved to France to escape persecution in the Soviet Union. Unfortunately he didn't suspect anyone like Hitler would come to power and take control of most of Europe."

"Was there much call for translators in France before the Nazis marched in?" Bolan inquired.

"About half my father's languages were so-called dead languages," Katz said with a smile. "Ancient Greek, Latin, Aramaic, old Celtic, that sort of thing. Needless to say, I don't know that he could really speak them all fluently."

"I don't know who could correct his accent," the Executioner commented. "So he mostly translated old documents, manuscripts and books?"

"Yes. Many of the translations were for the church. Diocese officials were frequent guests in our home. During the Crusades, Catholic clergy used to hire Jewish translators to decipher Arabic and Greek texts brought back from the Holy Land. It became sort of an old tradition. My father enjoyed it. Before the War, he also used to make trips to Germany and work for some of the publishers in Frankfurt."

"Sounds like he was a hell of a guy," Bolan remarked.

"He was a very kind and gentle man who believed one day people would learn to get along by communicating more freely with one another," Katz said fondly. "That's why he taught me English, German and Russian, as well as French, as soon as I was old enough to talk. I think I was about five years old when he added Hebrew to the curriculum. The best way to learn the proper accent for a language is to start learning when you're young. I didn't learn Arabic until I was in Palestine, and my accent is still a bit shaky."

"I don't think it is," Bolan assured him, "judging from what I've heard about how you handled communications and interrogations in the Middle East."

"I sometimes wonder what my father would think of what I've been using my language skills for," Katz said thoughtfully. "Certainly not what he had in mind when he first taught me another tongue."

"I think your father would be very proud of you, Yakov," the Executioner said softly.

Hal Brognola entered the War Room with a bundle of file folders under one arm and a computer printout sheet in his other hand. The Fed raised his eyebrows when he saw the two men.

"Hi, Yakov," Brognola greeted him, nodding as he moved to the head of the table. "I'm surprised you're still here, Mack."

"Did I wear out my welcome?" Bolan replied dryly. "I guess Grimaldi has the chopper ready. I haven't seen Yakov for some time, and we were just catching up a bit. Did you know Katz is working on his Italian, as well as the six languages he already knows?"

"Actually I'm only semifluent in Spanish and I'm working on it, as well as Turkish, Polish, Greek and Czech." Yakov grinned.

"How's your Indonesian?" Brognola asked as he took a cigar from his breast pocket.

"I'm afraid I overlooked that one," Katz admitted.

"Too bad," the Fed said as he removed the wrapper. "James and Manning are in the building and should be here any second now. Sorry to chase you outta here, Mack, but you know the rules we made when we first started this circus."

"Yeah," Bolan replied, nodding. "In fact, you shouldn't have even mentioned Indonesian while I was still in the room. Sure makes it clear Phoenix Force isn't headed for Northern Ireland in the near future."

"Uh . . . well, I never claimed to be perfect," Brognola said, obviously embarrassed.

"Good thing," Bolan replied, smiling slightly. "It was good seeing you again, Yakov. If we ever get a chance between missions, maybe we can get together and swap stories."

"Only those that won't be a risk to national security," Katz added lightly.

"That may not leave us with too many stories to tell," Bolan said, and headed for the exit.

Calvin James and Gary Manning appeared at the door. The tall, lanky, black Chicago warrior stared at Bolan as if he had just rounded the corner and encountered his favorite movie star. James had replaced one of the original five members of Phoenix Force, Keio Ohara, after the Japanese commando was killed in the line of duty in the summer of 1984. The other men of the Force had known Bolan since Stony Man began and had even worked with him in the field. James had only met the legendary Executioner briefly on two previous occasions, and he was still in awe of him.

"Oh, jeez," James said awkwardly. "Hello, Mr. Bolan. Real glad to see you again, man."

"It's a pleasure to see you too, Cal," Bolan assured him. "Just don't call me 'Mr. Bolan.' It makes my skin crawl!"

"Sorry," James said sheepishly. "Did you know I joined the San Francisco Police Department about six months after you did that number on those gangsters in Chinatown? Man, they were still talkin' about that. A hell of a lot of cops really thought what you did was bitchin' even if publicly they had to pretend they thought it was excessive vigilante action...."

"Cal, Mack is on his way out, and you guys are on your way in," Brognola announced. "Remember?"

"Yeah, I know," James said, clearly disappointed.

"Hell, Mack," Gary Manning remarked. "I guess the only way we'll see you for very long is if we get another mission together."

"Sounds good to me," James declared, eager to work with his longtime hero.

"Maybe next time," Bolan assured him, and clapped a hand across James's shoulder. "You guys watch your asses out there."

"Sure."

Bolan left the War Room. Manning and James joined Katz and Brognola at the table. The black badass from the Windy City shook his head and groaned.

"Did I really sound like an idiot just now?"

"Hell," Manning replied. "We were all pretty impressed by Bolan when we first met him. When you get to work with and really get to know him, you find out he's a human being and not some kind of god. That's when you're *really* impressed by the guy."

"McCarter's flight from England must have been delayed," Brognola stated. "Encizo was in the Caribbean doing some scuba diving or spearfishing or something like that. He's been contacted, and they're both on their way here. You guys will have to brief them when they arrive."

Manning headed for the coffeemaker and poured himself a cup of strong, black brew. The big Canadian quietly took a seat next to James and waited for Brognola to begin the briefing.

"You guys remember that big mission about a year ago?" the Fed began. "Started in Antarctica and wound up in the Philippines?"

"None of us will ever forget that one!" Katz replied. "I think I can safely speak for all of us when I say I sincerely hope you're not going to send us to Antarctica again."

"No, no," Brognola assured him, "but don't get too relaxed just yet. During that mission you guys briefly spent some time in the Molucca Islands. An officer in the Indonesian paratroopers helped you while you were there...."

"Major Tukarno," Katz said with a nod. "He's a good man. Helped us on a raid at a harbor."

"How do you remember all these wierd names?" Brognola asked after riffling through his files to find Katz had recalled the Indonesian officer's name and rank correctly. "Oh, I was wrong about Tukarno being a paratrooper. It says here he's with the PMB, or the Police Mobile Brigade, but he's qualified as a police parachutist. That's a new one for me. I didn't know you had to jump out of a plane to be a cop in Indonesia."

"The PMB is an elite military outfit and serves as Indonesia's antiterrorist unit, as well," Manning volunteered. The Canadian relayed the information as if it were common knowledge and took another sip of coffee.

"Yeah, that's right," Brognola commented as he read more from the file. "It seems like anything one of you fellas doesn't know, another one does."

"Not quite," Katz said. "We still don't know what our mission is."

Brognola explained what he had learned during his meeting with the President. The three Phoenix commandos listened gravely. Katz opened a pack of Camel cigarettes with the steel hooks at the end of his prosthesis and shook out a cigarette.

"Well, Indonesia is part of Southeast Asia," James remarked. "And it's a volatile region any way you look at it. With Vietnam, Laos and Cambodia nearby, I can see why NSA would want a listening post in Borneo. The Communist rebel forces and pro-Marcos supporters in the Philippines are two opposite sides of the old totalitarian coin in that country."

"That's not including the possibility that Indonesia itself might become a Communist nation if some people have their way," Brognola added. "*Glasnost*, smash-nost, the Reds are still the other side. We all hope the Soviet Union and the East European countries and maybe even Vietnam will adopt more democratic reforms so they eventually become more agreeable and less threatening. I don't think we'd be too worried if they all wound up like Yugoslavia, but after what happened in China, we've seen how quickly the Communist worm can turn. Indonesia has the fifth-largest population in the world. Uncle Sam would get real nervous if they were ruled by a Commie government."

"So we'll be working with Tukarno and the Police Mobile Brigade," Katz reminded him as he blew a smoke ring toward the ceiling. It almost reached the air conditioner vent before it dissolved. "I'm sure you've considered the possibility that whoever the enemy might be, if they've got inside information on NSA and CIA operations in Indonesia, they may well have connections within the government and the PMB."

"Oh, yeah," Brognola assured him. "That's why you'll be dealing directly with Tukarno, and he'll handle security personally. You'll also be accompanied by Amir Said. He's a native-born Indonesian who worked with the CIA in the late 1970s as a cutout. I got his file here. It looks pretty good. Seems the main reason he worked with the Company was because he wanted to come to the United States to become an American citizen. CIA was impressed with his work in the field and his dedication, so they cut some red tape so he could immigrate without the usual kilo of shit. He's been a naturalized U.S. citizen since 1985."

"Is he still with the Company?" Manning asked.

"Not really. They use him for courier missions from time to time. Most people wouldn't suspect a guy of Southeast Asian bloodline would be working for the CIA. When he's not working for Uncle Sam, Said runs a special electronics shop that deals mostly in eavesdropping devices for insurance investigators, private investigators and other snoops."

"Sounds like he could be a real asset," Katz said. "Does he still have connections in Indonesia?"

"Yeah," Brognola answered. "Some of them are probably involved in business that isn't entirely legal. Sometimes you have to deal with the guys in the sewers to get after the real big-league scum. Of course, you fellas know how things work as well as I do, maybe better."

"Well, I guess we'd better get our gear ready and pack some goodies for David and Rafael, as well," James commented. "As soon as they arrive, we'll meet up with this Said dude and be on our way. I wonder if Said might be related to a fellow I knew in Chicago named 'Say What.'"

"Oh, God," Manning muttered. "Don't make jokes about the man's name!"

"Hey," James said as he held up his hands in mock surrender, "I just wanted to get it out of my system now before I meet the guy."

3

Hasan Djarios peered down at the oil refinery from his perch atop a telephone pole. Dressed in gray work clothes, yellow helmet and tool belt, he looked like an employee of the phone company. From a distance no one would suspect that he was actually cutting the circuits to the cable control box. He finished severing all the lines to the refinery and closed the lid to the box.

A network of pipes connected the great concrete domes that contained the crude oil within the complex. Hundreds of kiloliters of petroleum pumped through the pipes from section to section, undergoing the chemical transformations that would prepare the product for market. The majority of the oil would not remain in Indonesia, Hasan Djarios thought bitterly. Most would be shipped to the United States or Western Europe.

He raised a pair of binoculars to his eyes and scanned the refinery from his vantage point. Most of the workers were locals. Sumatrans of the Batak and Achinese ethnic groups, they were slight, dark men with lean faces and Asian features. The engineers and supervisors were Malay-Chinese and Caucasian. This fact stirred Djarios's anger and resentment.

The executive manager was a white American named Peter Waldo. The Djarios brothers and the other members of *Mérah Tentera* had been studying him for more than a month. They knew where he lived, where his wife shopped and which school his children attended. They also knew the oil company Waldo worked for had assigned two bodyguards to protect the plant manager. One company executive had been kidnapped and killed in the Middle East, and there had been threats against the lives of several other personnel abroad. Waldo's bodyguards were originally a precaution that had only seemed necessary during the recent anti-American incidents in Indonesia.

Djarios spotted Waldo among the figures at the refinery. The tall pale man with thinning blond hair was easily recognizable even from a distance. He and his bodyguards had emerged from the office building to meet men arriving at the plant in a black limousine. More oil company executives from the United States. They were at the plant for some sort of inspection. *Mérah Tentera* had not been able to learn the exact reason the visitors were at the plant, but such details didn't matter.

Hasan descended the pole. Munap Djarios, his brother, waited by the bottom. Several other *Mérah Tentera* members were positoned by a green-and-white van with a phone company logo on each side of it. A small forest of banyans and palm trees blocked them from view from the plant.

"Did you cut off the phone lines, Hasan?" Munap asked eagerly as he gripped the ox-horn handle of the kris thrust in his belt.

"That was easy enough," his brother replied. "The other Americans have arrived. We must assume there are more bodyguards among them. They'll be armed, and the plant security personnel have weapons, as well."

"We've never objected to a good fight," Munap said with a grin.

Hasan grunted. He was two years older than Munap and less eager to charge into battle without knowing the odds. Munap's broad features glowed at the prospect of combat. He was a large man by Indonesian standards, physically powerful and a skilled fighter. He still favored the big kris with its long blade and wavy double-edged steel. Munap took great pride in his ability with the traditional Indonesian weapon.

Munap smiled as he handed his brother a *penjut* whip. Hasan could not resist a smile in return. The *penjut* was Hasan's favorite weapon, and his skill with it equaled his brother's ability with his knife. Hasan was slightly smaller and less muscular than Munap. He was also less willing to battle an opponent at close quarters and trade blows in a fight. Munap prided himself on his ability to absorb punishment and, thanks to years of training in the deadly martial art of *mustika kwitang*, he could kill a man with a single blow. By contrast, Hasan's fighting style was *tjingrik*, which emphasizes speed and cunning.

"The operation will continue as planned," Hasan told the others. "We will be faced with more opponents than expected, but the number is not great enough for us to delay until a more favorable time. Everyone knows what he is to do?"

The others affirmed that they were ready.

"Good," Hasan said. "Let us begin."

THE VAN PULLED UP to the steel wire gates at the front of the oil refinery. Two security guards watched the vehicle closely. They were aware that outside telephone lines were out of order. The visiting Americans had already tried unsuccessfully to make an overseas call to New York City to report that they had arrived. They had complained to Mr. Soe, the assistant manager, who in turn had complained to security. Management was always ready to blame security for anything that went wrong with the plant.

The refinery was located near the coast, not far from the oil derricks along the Berhala Strait. Djambi was the only city of any size within the area. The few public services used by the plant were supplied by Djambi. Sumatra is hardly a center for modern conveniences, even by Indonesian standards.

One of the sentries entered a shack and pressed the button to the control panel to the gate. It slid open with an electrical hum, and the van rolled forward across the threshold. The other security guard moved in front of the vehicle and held up a hand to urge it to stop.

"We found some damaged phone lines about four kilometers from here," Hasan announced as he stuck his head out the window at the driver's side of the van. "Has anyone reported trouble with their phones here?"

"There have been many complaints," the guard confirmed. "I saw someone on a telephone pole in the distance. Was he one of your people?"

"In fact, it was I," Hasan said, honestly enough. "I repaired some of the damage, but other problems seem to be based here with your telephone system. With so many phones here and their constant use, our equipment can barely handle them sometimes."

"These Americans think they're still back in New York," the guard muttered. "We'll have to look in the back of your vehicle."

"Of course," Bagus assured him with a smile. A small man with an unusually large head, Bagus sat beside Hasan in the front seat. "We understand. You're just doing your job."

"The back door isn't locked," Hasan told the guard. "Please, help yourself."

"Terima kasih," the security man said with a short bow. "Thank you. I appreciate your cooperation."

The other sentry emerged from the shack and approached the van to check the identification of the "phone repairmen." Bagus looked at Hasan. The *Mérah Tentera* leader nodded and glanced at the bamboo tube in Bagus's right hand. As the guard drew closer, Bagus raised the *sumpit*, or blowgun, to his lips and exhaled hard into the mouthpiece. The dart hissed from the tube and into the sentry's neck just below the jawline.

The man opened his mouth to cry out, but the curare-laced barb had already frozen his neck muscles. He barely groaned as he reached for the holstered pistol on his hip. Bagus took another dart from a shirt pocket and slipped it into the end of his *sumpit*. However, the guard's fingers merely twitched at the button-flap holster without opening it. He collapsed to the ground.

In the meantime, the other guard was opening the van's rear door. Munap Djarios stood inside, a Beretta Model 12 submachine gun in one fist and his kris knife in the other. The guard stared up at the unexpected figure, startled. Munap lashed out a boot and kicked him in the face. The man's head snapped back, and he staggered several steps back.

Munap pursued his advantage, jumping from the van and lunging at the sentry with his kris before the man toppled over. The steel tip pierced the hollow of the sentry's throat, and the wavy curved blade sliced flesh and muscle. Blood gushed from the wound as the guard's falling body pulled his throat from the blade. Munap watched the dying figure thrash about on the ground by his feet.

"Hey!" An American engineer dressed in work clothes and a yellow hard hat called out as he approached the van. "What the hell is going on?"

Hasan leaped from the vehicle and reached under the front seat to grab the handle of his *penjut*. He yanked the whip out and swung his arm as he stepped toward the engineer. The twisted leather snapped the air with a sharp crack like the report of a small-caliber pistol. It struck the startled foreigner across the side of his face and wrapped around his head like the black tentacle of a monstrous and vengeful squid.

The engineer uttered a stifled moan, the hard leather cord jammed between his teeth. The whip still held his skull in its vicelike grip as Hasan yanked the captive toward him. The hard hat barely protected part of the engineer's head from the punishing blow of the lash.

Hasan stepped closer and kicked viciously at the American's groin. The engineer gasped in agony as he doubled up, violently wheezing. Hasan did not give him time to recover. He hammered the copper-capped butt of the whip's handle into the American's neck just where the shoulder and neck meet behind the collarbone. The engineer fell to his knees, stunned and paralyzed. To finish the job Hasan yanked the hard hat from his head and smashed the whip handle into the base of his skull. The engineer collapsed face-first to the ground.

Not a shot had been fired, and most of the personnel in the refinery hadn't heard the crack of Hasan's *penjut*. The machinery in the plant produced enough noise to mask most other sounds. Only a handful of workers noticed the van and the activity at the front gate. Then, several armed figures ran through the open entrance while Munap Djarios stood watch by the guard shack, Beretta subgun in his fists.

"Bahaja!" more than one Indonesian employee cried out. "Danger! Look out!"

Peter Waldo and one of his bodyguards stared down from a second-story window of the office building just in time to see the invaders rush into the refinery. Waldo swung away and reached for a telephone on a desktop, recalling as he did so that the outside lines were not working. The other American executives were unaware of what had happened outside, but all the bodyguards suspected something serious had occurred.

"Everybody stay away from the windows," Waldo's protector ordered as he reached inside his jacket for a .357 Magnum in shoulder leather. "It looks like we're under attack."

The roar of automatic weapons outside the building confirmed his words. The *Mérah Tentera* forces knew the general layout of the refinery. Uniformed figures appeared at various corners of the plant, and the terrorists immediately opened fire on the guards. Guards tumbled to the ground before they could even pull out their pistols.

The invaders were better armed than the security personnel. Hasan, Munap and the others carried M-16 and Beretta BM59 assault rifles and M-12 submachine guns. Most of the guards were only armed with handguns. One security man managed to grab a 12-gauge pump shotgun from his station and duck behind the limousine for cover. He poked the riot gun around the side of the big black car and squeezed the trigger. A burst of buckshot bashed in the chest of one of the *Mérah Tentera* killers. The terrorist was jerked off his feet for three meters and crashed to the ground in a bleeding, ravaged lump.

"Munap!" Hasan shouted to his brother as he pulled a hand grenade from his belt. "The car!"

He yanked the pin from the grenade. Munap trained his Beretta chopper on the limo while Hasan dropped low and hurled the grenade in an underhand toss. It skidded across the ground and under the limousine. The massive explosion blasted the belly of the automobile and blew off tires and doors. The guard was thrown from his shelter, his clothes torn and body bloodied.

Munap fired at the injured figure. Nine-millimeter slugs smashed into the guard and kicked his corpse across the ground. Movement among the oil pipes above drew Munap's attention. He raised the Beretta and sprayed another salvo at a pair of men among the pipes. Both were unarmed laborers. Munap calmly watched the pair twitch from the force of multiple 9 mm rounds. They deserved whatever punishment they received for working for the Americans. One man's corpse plunged from the peak to crash to the ground below. The other body slumped across a pipe like a grisly decoration.

Hasan jogged to the office building, accompanied by Bagus and another terrorist. They pulled the pins from grenades and lobbed the explosives through windows at both first and second-story levels. A trio of blasts erupted almost simultaneously, glass spewing from the shattered windows. Plaster dust and chunks of furniture burst from the openings.

Munap and another terrorist charged through the front door to the office building. Debris was strewn across the bloodied and battered figures inside the rooms. Papers were scattered everywhere amid the remains of desks and other furniture. An electrical fire had started at the terminal board of a computer, its wiring ripped apart by a grenade blast.

The *Mérah Tentera* gunmen sprayed the fallen employees with automatic weapons to ensure that they were dead.

Munap and his companion watched the high-velocity bullets tear into the still forms. In a businesslike manner they removed the spent magazines from their weapons, reloaded and headed for the stairwell.

On the second floor they discovered the offices were in a condition similar to those below. Munap kicked in the door to the executive conference room, and his companion shuffled in with an M-16 braced against a hip. The room had been demolished. Peter Waldo's corpse lay pinned under a desk. The terrorist grunted with satisfaction and spit on the dead man.

He didn't notice the figure behind the desk until the bodyguard leaned around the furniture to aim his .357 at him. The big revolver snarled in the confines of the conference room. The bodyguard fired both Magnum rounds through the gunman's chest. He saw his opponent fall, but his own eardrums had been ruptured by the explosion, and he didn't hear Munap's Beretta subgun. A column of 9 mm parabellum rounds split him open from breastbone to throat.

The revolver hopped from the bodyguard's grasp as the force of the bullets drove him across the room. The man stumbled over another corpse and crashed to the floor. Munap glanced at his fallen comrade and saw there was nothing he could do for him. The *Mérah Tentera* soldier had been shot through the heart.

"You bastard!" a voice snarled from a filing cabinet to the right of Munap.

The big Indonesian turned and glimpsed another bodyguard charge from the cover of the cabinets. The American dragged one leg as he forced himself forward as fast as he could go. His left arm was also broken, and his face was cut and bruised, but he lunged fiercely at Munap and swung an electric fan in his right fist.

The fan struck the frame of Munap's Beretta. The bodyguard's attack had been awkward but desperate, and he struck with the furious strength of a man with nothing to lose. The blow sent the Beretta flying from Munap's grasp. The bodyguard raised the fan a second time in a backhand sweep aimed at Munap's skull.

The terrorist suddenly snap-kicked his opponent in the gut and grabbed his wrist with one hand and the elbow with the other. Munap twisted the captive limb forcibly until the fan fell from the American's fingers. Then the Indonesian applied a straight-arm bar hold to lock the arm and slashed a hand across the elbow. The bone cracked, and the bodyguard screamed as the elbow joint popped like a piece of kindling.

Snarling, Munap grabbed his opponent's head in both hands. The Yankee had startled him, embarrassed him by getting the better of him when he was off guard. Now he was helpless and completely at Munap's mercy. With both arms and one leg broken, the American could do nothing to defend himself as Munap dragged him across the room.

The Indonesian bellowed with rage as he hammered his opponent's head into a wall. The plaster caved in from the blows, and the blood stained the surface with each blow. Munap rammed a knee into the American's abdomen as he continued to bash the man's head into the wall again and again. He stared at the smashed and blood-streaked face and raised one arm high. His bent elbow crashed down into his opponent's skull just above the hairline. Bone cracked sickeningly, and the bodyguard finally slumped lifeless at Munap's feet.

"Is that the last of them, Munap?" Hasan inquired as he appeared at the doorway.

"Scum," Munap hissed as he kicked the corpse. "One of them killed Sejech, but I took care of that Yankee son of a whore, as well."

"Waldo and the other oil company executives are dead," Hasan commented. "That is what matters. Come, my brother. We must get out of here."

4

"They do have Coca-Cola in Indonesia, don't they?" David McCarter asked hopefully as he turned from the window seat of the Boeing 707 to face Amir Said.

"In Djakarta and many other major cities," Said replied, surprised by the question. "Some of the small towns in Bali sell American soft drinks since tourists are usually more interested in seeing Bali. It has a rather exotic reputation."

"I just hope we don't spend too much time far from anywhere that sells Coke," McCarter commented, and fired up a Player's cigarette. "That's the cola I mean, not the nose candy."

Said smiled. The tall, lean Briton's sly features reminded him of a clever young fox that could always outwit the hounds. His accent was similar to the English of Australians Said had known in the past. A Cockney accent. That meant McCarter came from the East End of London. That part of the city had a reputation for being tough, and it tended to produce tough men.

"Collins has a great fondness for Coca-Cola," Gary Manning explained as he studied a map of the Indonesian islands. "We try to make sure he has his Coke and cigarettes to calm him down until we're ready to turn him loose on the battlefield."

"You make me sound like a mental case, Miller," the Briton complained.

"Well?" Manning replied with a shrug.

McCarter made a rude gesture with two erect fingers. The American version of this same gesture uses one finger instead of two. Manning simply smiled, pleased that he had got a response from the Briton.

"Come on, you guys," Calvin James urged with mock concern in his voice. "Let's not be uncouth and make a bad impression on Mr. Said."

"Just call me Amir," Said declared. "My last name does sound a bit strange to people who speak English. I've heard lots of jokes about it since I became an American citizen."

"Really?" James asked innocently.

Said was aware that he was the only man among the group using his real name. The others called themselves "Collins," "Miller," "Colby," "Jones" and "Ramirez," but Said knew these were false identities for the mission. He did not know about Phoenix Force or who these five men really were, but he did know their security clearance was top level. They also had enough connections with the U.S. government and other governments throughout the world to cut through red tape like a laser beam through cardboard.

"Actually Mr. Collins is wise to drink cola or bottled water," Said stated. "In fact, I suggest none of you drink any water unless it has been boiled. Coffee and tea are all right if the water is boiled well. Milk is safe to drink in some places, but please check with me before you do so."

"See?" McCarter said defensively. "I told you blokes it was smart to drink Coca-Cola."

McCarter had acquired his taste for Coke after spending time in Vietnam as a "special oberver" and later serving with the SAS in Oman, where Communist rebels in the Dhofar region tended to poison waterholes.

"So we have to watch out for the water, too," Rafael Encizo commented as he rubbed his left arm. "I still feel like the victim of an deranged porcupine from all the shots Jones gave me."

"We all got 'em," James told him. "Smallpox, cholera, typhoid, paratyphoid and yellow fever inoculations are health insurance for Indonesia. Yellow fever isn't all that likely, but I threw it in just to be sure. Last time we got shots for it was when we were last in Africa. Figured it was time for some booster shots."

"More likely just a streak of sadism on your part," Encizo muttered.

Of course, the Cuban knew better. Encizo and the others trusted Calvin James's judgment on any and all medical matters. James had been a hospital corpsman when he was with the Seals in the Navy and he had continued his education in medicine and battlefield surgery since his tour of duty in Vietnam. He was the Phoenix Force unit medic.

Encizo had been the last member of Phoenix Force to arrive at the airstrip near Arlington, so he had received the inoculations most recently. The pain of the needle was actually no big deal to the tough Cuban. He was a veteran of the Bay of Pigs invasion and had endured torture in a Cuban political prison. Complaining about the shots was just a way of making conversation during the long flight to Indonesia.

It was a long and indirect flight. They had flown from the United States to the Marshall Islands in the Pacific, to Australia and then on to Indonesia. This was to avoid having their flight directly connected with the U.S. Phoenix Force did not know if the mysterious "other side" were watching the airports for flights arriving from the U.S. or if they had informers within the American Embassy, NSA or CIA.

Yakov Katzenelenbogen turned to face Amir Said. The Indonesian was less than one hundred sixty-five centimeters tall, yet his long torso and limbs created an illusion of greater height. Said's features were pleasant, with an easy smile and intelligent dark Asian eyes. He had white, capped teeth, something he had accomplished after becoming a U.S. citizen, and he wore his long black hair combed straight back from his sleek head. Said did not look cunning or dangerous, but Katz had read the man's file and realized Amir Said was no stranger to intrigue or violence.

"When was the last time you visited Indonesia, Amir?" Katz asked as he reached for an Indonesian phrasebook on the seat beside him.

"Three years ago," Said answered. "I attended my mother's funeral. She was the last member of my immediate family in Indonesia. My brother lives in Singapore, and my older sister married a lawyer in Hong Kong. My younger sister also moved to the U.S. and works as a dental assistant in Sacramento. I still have friends and relatives in Java, Sumatra and Borneo. A couple of them are involved in trade—smuggling and black market. No drugs or prostitution, and none of them would ever assist any sort of terrorist outfit. Especially not Communists."

"I've never been too much for trusting crooks," James admitted.

"They're trustworthy," Said assured him. "They also have sources of information the police and the intelligence people don't have. They've helped me before, and we may need them."

"Maybe we should have contacted them to smuggle in our weapons and other gear," Encizo remarked. "Since we couldn't use one of the Embassy's diplomatic pouches or arrange to have customs waived, we'll have to make do with whatever Major Tukarno can supply us with."

"Yeah," Manning agreed. "None of us like using weapons we're not familiar with or haven't used on the firing range. We like to know how accurate a weapon is and the exact rate of fire. Just how natural a weapon feels in your hands can make a big difference in a firefight."

"I have an uncle who might be able to get you some firearms," Said offered. "Mostly black-market arms from Australia and the Philippines. Too bad you don't need knives, chains and staves. Getting those wouldn't be any problem."

"Those are weapons used with that Indonesian style of karate, right?" James inquired. "Or is it more similar to Chinese *chuan fa*? What's incorrectly called kung fu in the States."

"We call it *pentjak-silat*," Said replied. "It's similar to other martial arts in some ways, but the techniques are different from other Asian styles. For one thing, it is taught exclusively for self-defense and there are no belt colors or *dan* ranks. In *pentjak-silat* one is taught to use conventional weapons and whatever happens to be at hand in an emergency. Style can vary dramatically from one area to another and even one village to another."

"And you've studied these arts?" Manning asked.

"Three different styles," Said confirmed with a nod. "Each time I went to a guru, or teacher, and brought the traditional items. You're expected to bring a small amount of money to pay for the instructor's clothes if they're ripped during practice and some tobacco for him to smoke during rest periods. A knife and a chicken are for symbolic reasons. The sharp edge of the knife represents the sharpness demanded of the student, and the chicken is given as a sacrifice so that its blood may be shed instead of a person's during training. The student is also required to bring a white sheet, of course."

"A sheet?" James asked with raised eyebrows. "What's that for?"

"In case the student is killed during training," Said explained. "Then his corpse is wrapped in the sheet as a shroud."

"Sounds like you blokes have some tough training," McCarter remarked.

"Not too many students actually get killed," Said assured him. "It is taken seriously, of course. Unlike judo or karate, *pentjak-silat* is never regarded as a sport. Most of the instructors are Muslim, so the student has to swear an oath of the Koran that he will never abuse his knowledge and skills or use them for evil."

"Interesting mixture of cultures in Indonesia," Katz, with his degree in archaeology, remarked. "I must admit the language has me puzzled. I've been trying to learn a few expressions in Indonesian, but it seems to have words and character traits from both Asian and European languages. Teutonic languages, at that. For example, the word for 'yes' is *ja*."

"There are more than a hundred languages spoken in Indonesia, but Bahasa Indonesian is the official language," Said explained. "You're right about it being a mixture. Indonesian is based on Malay, but it has been influenced by Chinese, Hindi, Urdu and Dutch, with a bit of English, as well. The Dutch influence dates back to the seventeenth century and continued until the government of the Netherlands relinquished sovereignty to all of Indonesia in 1949. Not surprisingly it also influenced the language."

"I wonder what's influencing the bleedin' terrorists," McCarter commented as he reached for his pack of Player's.

The warning lights blinked on and instructed the six passengers to buckle their seatbelts and refrain from smoking. The Briton reluctantly put his cigarettes away as Phoenix Force and Amir Said waited for the plane to land.

MAJOR TUKARNO MET them at the Djakarta Airport. It was easy to spot the little Qantas Airways 707 among the Garuda Indonesian Airways commercial craft. Tukarno had no trouble recognizing the five incredible commandos he had met a year ago at an obscure airfield in the Moluccas. They were not the sort of men one ever forgets.

Phoenix Force, one the other hand, had a little more trouble recognizing the major. Tukarno was dressed in a poorly fitting tan suit and gray necktie instead of a uniform. As uncomfortable as he felt in civilian clothes, he stood with ramrod straight posture, his head held high. He had the manner of a man accustomed to commanding others.

A short, stocky figure stood beside the slender military officer. Had Phoenix Force not met Sergeant Jatta before, they may have guessed from his flat features and heavy brow that he was dull witted or brutish. In fact, Tukarno's aide was an unusually intelligent man, well-read and fluent in at least three languages.

"I'm glad to see you all arrived safely," Tukarno greeted them with a slight bow. "None too soon, I must say. We need to get your luggage and leave immediately."

"It sounds as if something has happened we don't know about," Katz remarked. "Another problem, I assume."

"A rather large problem," Tukarno confirmed.

The visitors passed customs with their expertly forged identification papers and passports. They carried nothing but their simple carry-on luggage and soon left the airport with the two military men. Tukarno escorted them to a dark blue delivery truck with the legend *Penén Rumah* painted on the side. There was ample room for all five commandos, Amir Said and Major Tukarno inside. Jatta climbed into the driver's seat.

The passengers sat on benches as Tukarno switched on an overhead light. There were no windows inside the box-like rear of the vehicle, but it was air-conditioned and pleasantly cool. Tukarno explained that the truck was formerly used by *Penén Rumah* restaurant. When the establishment had gone out of business, the Police Mobile Brigade had made a deal with the Indonesian Security Council to use the building for their undercover surveillance operations. Phoenix Force would be using it for a safe house during their mission.

As the truck rolled forward, the major told them about the attack on the oil refinery in Sumatra. The operations had been carried out swiftly and effectively with brutal ruthlessness. Twenty-eight people had been killed during the attack, not including the two terrorist corpses left behind. The American oil executives had been the obvious main targets of the invaders, but they evidently showed no hesitation in killing anyone else who got in their way, regardless of nationality.

"We don't know who the terrorists are this time," the major continued. "*Mérah Tentera* is our leading suspect."

"It means 'Red Army,' Said translated. "They're a Marxist-Leninist extremist outfit more or less modeled after the old Japanese Red Army. *Mérah Tenetera* has quite a reputation for violence and hit-and-run tactics, but

I didn't think they showed much effort at strategy or real organizational skills in the past."

"That's what we think, too," Tukarno said, and cast a curious glance at Amir Said. "You have experience in this field?"

"I wouldn't be here otherwise," Said replied.

"No," Tukarno said thoughtfully. "I suppose you wouldn't be. You're quite right about *Mérah Tentera*. In fact, we had thought they had been pretty well wiped out until now. The attacks resemble *Mérah Tentera* tactics because of their excessive violence and complete disregard for killing innocent bystanders. And the decapitations fit their style. However, the obvious planning involved in these attacks demonstrates some military expertise and some sort of recon and intelligence work that doesn't fit with their past behavior. I believe the police in your country call it an M.O.?"

"Modus operandi," Calvin James confirmed with a nod. The tough black dude had formerly been a member of the San Francisco SWAT team. "So maybe the local version of the Red Army isn't responsible, or maybe they've gone through renovations and they're back in the business under a new management."

"It's too soon for us to come up with any valid theories," Katz stated. "Are the PMB and local authorities investigating?"

"My unit is involved in the investigation," Tukarno answered. "The Police Mobile Brigade is largely concerned with anti-terrorism and protecting national security. The locals in Sumatra are investigating, as well, but the PMB is a national government branch so we outrank them. The American Embassy has sent some security personnel to look into it, too. Apparently they're already claiming jurisdiction because the attack occurred at a U.S.-

owned refinery and many of the victims were American citizens.''

"Embassy security," Encizo said with contempt. "In other words it's CIA."

"Sounds like the Company," Said agreed. "It could be NSA. Neither one is very good at investigating crimes."

"Intelligence organizations are designed to get information other people don't want them to get and to conceal their own secrets from the opposition," Katz stated. "CIA and NSA probably don't have many qualified personnel here in Indonesia to help with criminal investigations and forensics. The Company will probably try to get as much as they can from the PMB and local police. They might try to bully you with claims that they represent the United States government. NSA will be more likely to plug into your police computers and try to get information that way. The National Security Agency also has a very large network in Australia and New Zealand. They'll probably recruit personnel from those sections with expertise in criminal investigation fields."

"But you're not working with the American intelligence organizations?" Tukarno inquired. "That's what I understood. That's why I haven't contacted the U.S. Embassy personnel."

"Absolutely right," Katz confirmed. "Since NSA agents were among the murder victims, we can't be sure if they were killed because their cover was burned. If that's the case, NSA and probably CIA have a major security leak here. There's no point in us working with them if everything we do might be leaked to the enemy."

"Maybe we could convince the bastards to come after us," McCarter suggested. "Lure them out from under their bloody rocks to fight us. It'd be easier if we can get the buggers to come to us."

"I know that idea appeals to you," Katz said with a sigh, "but I doubt it would work. They'd probably be more inclined to avoid a confrontation with us than to eagerly welcome a fight."

"Speaking of fights," Encizo began, "we need some hardware, Major. Did you get some weapons for us?"

"At the restaurant," Tukarno assured him. "I wasn't sure what you'd need, so I have military weapons of American, Soviet, British, German, Danish, Italian and Swedish manufacture."

"Jesus," Manning rasped. "How'd you get such a range of weapons so quickly?"

"That's Indonesia," Said commented. "The military here uses an incredible variety of small arms from all different sources. Some of the soldiers and police still carry Tokarev pistols, believe it or not. Troops might carry anything from a British .303 rifle to a Russian SKS carbine."

"You sound rather critical," the major said stiffly.

"I'd just hate to be in a gun battle armed with a .45 pistol and run out of ammunition when the other men I'm with only have spare ammo in 9 mm or 7.62 mill," Said replied.

"We'd better take a look at what you've got and figure out what will work best for us," Katz declared.

"I just hope you've got at least one Browning Hi-Power," McCarter declared gruffly. "If you don't, I might just turn around and go home."

"Gee," Gary Manning said with a raised eyebrow. "You promise?"

The Briton replied with another hand signal.

5

Phoenix Force saw little of Djakarta as they traveled through the capital of Indonesia in the back of the windowless delivery truck. The vehicle finally came to a halt in an alley next to the *Penén Rumah* restaurant. Sergeant Jatta walked around to the rear to open the door.

Major Tukarno led the five commandos and Amir Said to a side door of the building. A man inside opened the door and stepped aside to let the others enter. He was young and thin, dressed in a fatigue uniform with the dark blue beret and red scarf of the Police Mobile Brigade. Gold chevrons on his sleeve marked him as a sergeant first class, and the insignia at his left shoulder displayed the eagle head and lightning bolt of the PMB.

"Gentlemen," Major Tukarno began, "this is Sergeant Mudo. He's a computer technician, among other things, and maintains our link with headquarters and the security council. He also speaks English."

"It's a fairly common second language in Indonesia," Mudo said with a shrug. "Information has arrived from Sumatra, Major. The dead terrorists are being fingerprinted, and we're hoping there will be a positive ID on at least one of them. There are also some interesting details about some of the dead workers and executives at the plant. The manager was a man named Waldo. His right hand was missing. They say from the appearance of the clean cut at the wrist, it had been..."

He stopped in midsentence and stared at the steel hooks at the end of Katz's right arm. The Israeli smiled. He was accustomed to his reaction, but it was rather ironic under the circumstances.

"I'm not Waldo," he assured Mudo.

"Of course not, sir," the sergeant said awkwardly. "Uh...there were also some unusual weapons used. One victim was killed by a poison dart, apparently fired from a blowgun. A couple were stabbed. Survivors mentioned that at least one terrorist was armed with a whip."

"I hope they managed to give some descriptions of the attackers?" Manning inquired.

"Doesn't seem too helpful so far," Mudo answered. "They are all vague. Descriptions could fit almost anyone. It all happened quite quickly. The workers were more concerned with staying alive than with identifying their attackers."

"Understandably," James commented as he glanced around the kitchen.

The large professional ovens and freezer unit had not been removed. Television monitors were set along a table. Cameras and microphones outside the building allowed Mudo or whoever was on duty to check the place for unwanted intruders or surveillance by others.

"I really need a 9 mm security blanket," McCarter announced. "Say what you want, but I feel mighty uncomfortable unarmed."

"Yeah," Encizo agreed. "Can we see those guns now?"

"There's nothing to worry about here," Mudo assured them. "This building is quite secure."

"Past experience has taught us no place is entirely secure," Katz told the NCO. "The only real security you have is the personal security of being able to defend yourself in the most efficient manner."

"Sergeant Jatta," Tukarno spoke to his aide, "please show them the arms room."

"Please follow me," Jatta told Phoenix Force.

He escorted the five warriors and Amir Said through the dining room. The tables and chairs had been moved to make room for bunk beds and desks. A computer terminal and display terminal were mounted on one desk, and a radio unit was set on another. Several wall lockers lined one side of the room. Two had padlocks on the doors. Jatta produced a key ring and unlocked the closest container.

The sergeant opened the doors. Inside was a gun rack loaded with a variety of automatic assault rifles. More than a dozen pistols were on the top shelf. Jatta moved to the second locker and opened it, revealing submachine guns and more handguns.

"I don't suppose you have any Uzi machine pistols or standard-size submachine guns?" Katz inquired.

"No. I'm afraid we don't have any Uzis or Israeli firearms of any sort," Jatta replied. "The Indonesian military generally use the Beretta M-12 submachine gun, but the PMB has been adopting the Heckler & Koch MP-5. The West German GSG-9 antiterrorist units have used this weapon for years. We've also found the MP-5 to be very reliable."

"I'm familiar with it," Manning said. He did not mention that he had actually served with a GSG-9 unit in the 1970s. "It's a fine weapon."

"Absolutely," Encizo agreed. The MP-5 had once been his standard assault weapon, and he liked and trusted firearms made by Heckler & Koch.

"I kinda favor the Beretta," James said with a sigh, "but we should all have the same subgun, so I'll go along with the H&K, too."

"Good," Katz said with a nod. "Now, about handguns. We generally use a Walther P-88, fifteen-shot, double-action 9 mm pistol."

"I don't," McCarter insisted. "I've used the Browning Hi-Power for nearly twenty years, and I'm bloody well sticking with it. Those fancy double-action autoloaders have more gizmos, and there's more that can go wrong with them. Give me a good old single-action 9 mm Browning any time."

"No problem, Mr. Collins," Jatta assured him as he reached into a locker and removed a blue-black pistol from a shelf. "This is a Browning Pindad, manufactured at the Fabrik Sendjata Ringan. Aside from the Pindad printed on the slide, you'll find it's identical to the Browning Hi-Power."

"Bloody lovely," McCarter announced as he took the pistol.

"Good," Manning growled. "Maybe now he'll shut up."

"We don't have any Walther P-88 pistols," Jatta admitted. "However, we do have a number of Beretta Model 92 double-action 9 mm pistols. They use a fifteen-shot magazine."

"It's a good gun. We'll go with it," said Katz. "We've all fired them on target ranges, if not in actual combat. What about you, Amir?"

"I've never fired one," Said confessed. "I'm basically a Colt .45 1911 shooter. The Browning uses a similar frame and it's a single-action auto, too. Better if I go with it."

"Fine," Katz agreed, "but you and Collins both have to understand that the rest of us won't carry spare magazines for the Browning."

"But I'll carry a spare Beretta mag for you blokes," McCarter said cheerfully as he stuck the Browning in his belt. "I don't need to carry a lot of spare ammunition for the Hi-Power. I don't miss very often."

None of the other Phoenix commandos would argue with McCarter. He was an exceptional pistol marksman, and had once belonged to the British Olympic pistol team. His accuracy with the Browning was the main reason the others did not object to his fetish for the single-action autoloader.

"For assault rifles we assumed you'd favor American-made M-16s," Jatta remarked, "but we also have some Soviet AK-47s and two Heckler & Koch G-3 rifles."

"I'll take the G-3," Manning announced. "It's 7.62 mm NATO caliber and designed similar to the FN FAL rifle. The only 5.56 mm weapon I have much faith in is the British SAR-80."

"Mr. Miller is our top rifle marksman," Katz explained. "He gets what he wants. I'm a poor rifle shot because of my prosthesis and my hand-eye coordination. Is the M-16 okay with the rest of you?"

"Damn straight," James agreed. "Especially if I can have an M-203 grenade launcher attached to the barrel of my weapon and some 40 mm cartridge-style grenades to go with it."

"We can manage that," Jatta confirmed. "We also have both American-made M-26 fragmentation grenades and Soviet F-1 grenades."

"What about tear gas and concussion grenades?" Encizo asked.

"We can get them," the sergeant replied.

"I'll need plastic explosives, as well," Manning said.

"Preferably Composition-Four, RDX compound, some British CV-38, low-velocity gelignite."

"We have a supply of C-4 here," Jatta answered. "I'm sure we can get the CV-38 for you, as well. Primacord, detonators and special blasting caps are also available."

"You fellows have done pretty well," Encizo remarked. "One more item we'll need are knives and maybe some garrotes."

"The traditional kris may be a bit awkward for them," Said commented.

"What about bayonets?" Jatta inquired. He had not expected Western commandos to be concerned with edged weapons.

"They're designed to go on rifle barrels," Encizo insisted. "What I'm used to is a *tanto* fighting knife. Actually a Cold Steel Tanto manufactured in Ventura, California. I guess that would be hoping for too much, so maybe a single-edged blade with high-quality steel and a reinforced tip. If it's designed like a samurai *tanto*, that's even better."

"I doubt I can find something like that," Jatta admitted. "In fact, I don't even know what a *tanto* is."

"The design of the knife is similar to a samurai sword," Encizo answered. "Maybe I can buy something in a shop that will suit me. I'd also like a dagger for a boot knife. Something similar to a Gerber Mark I?"

"I don't think you'll find that any more than I'll be able to find a Blackmoor Dirk or a Jackass Leather shoulder holster rig," Calvin James told him. "We'll have to settle for what we can get, man."

"I know a shop that sells some fine German and Spanish knives," Said announced. "I'll take you there, and you can buy what you like."

"I had no idea you fellows would be so fastidious," Major Tukarno remarked as he approached the commandos.

"When your life depends on your equipment," Katz said, "you tend to be very fastidious. Now that we've got basic weaponry taken care of, let's hear more about the incident at the refinery."

"Sergeant Mudo?" Tukarno began as he glanced about for the NCO.

"Data is coming in, Major," Mudo announced. He sat at the desk with the computer terminal. Yellow letters flashed across the green screen. "They managed to identify one of the dead terrorists."

Manning hurried to the computer, eager to see the information. He felt silly when he saw the data was written in Indonesian. The NCO translated as the messages rolled across the screen.

"Hitam, first name Sejech," Mudo read aloud. "Born in Malang, East Java, on February 2, 1967. Arrested for assault when he was sixteen and sentenced to five years at Ek Penjara."

"That's a prison in Java," Tukarno explained. "In fact, it's on an island in the Java Sea less than a hundred kilometers from Djakarta."

"Hitam's assault was directed against a Sekber Golkar member of the provincial legislative branch," Mudo added, still studying the screen. "It seems to have been politically motivated."

"Sekber Golkar is the largest political party in Indonesia," Tukarno explained. "It's also been the ruling party for the last twenty years."

"The government believes Hitam was a member of a Marxist student group when he committed the assault," Mudo continued to read. "However, he claimed to have been acting on his own, and he didn't cause any problems while in prison. He even repented for his crimes against society and promised to be a good citizen when he got out. He was released in 1988 and worked for a commercial fisherman named Chin Ho Li at Sindangbarang. That's a coastal city along the Indian Ocean in West Java. According to Chin, Hitam was a good employee until he just failed to show up for work one day and disappeared in late 1989.''

"That's about the same time the *Mérah Tentera* first appeared," Said remarked.

"We may have to check with Mr. Chin," Katz remarked. "That's a Chinese name, isn't it?"

"Probably Malay-Chinese," Said explained. "They're a large ethnic group in Indonesia."

"I'm also getting identification on the other dead terrorist," Mudo announced as more data appeared on the screen. "His name was Kampur, first name Yusaf. Born in Sumatra on April 3, 1968. Also had a criminal record. Vandalism and petty robbery when he was eighteen. Served two years in Ek Penjara."

"So he could have met Hitam while he was in the joint," James noted. "What about leftist politics?"

"Vandalized a Golkar party center in Palembang, Sumatra," Mudo confirmed. "After he was released from prison, Kampur worked for a rubber plantation near Rengat in Sumatra. He's still listed as employed there, according to the parole office."

"Maybe his employers and co-workers can tell us more about him," Encizo suggested.

"As leads go, it's not much, but it's better than nothing," Manning said. "How long will it take the local police and the PMB to get on this?"

"We can beat them to it," Tukarno assured him, "if we move quickly. The local authorities in Sumatra won't have this information until the authorities in Java see fit to share it with them. They'll have to get criminal investigators to the case and forensics lab personnel and whatever. Since I'm a field-grade officer in the PMB and I have top priority on this assignment, thanks to your influence with the White House and the President's influence on the Indonesian government, there won't be any problem."

"It'll take the NSA and CIA quite a bit longer," Said assured the others. "They're probably getting in each other's way right now."

"And paying more attention to keeping information from each other than checking into leads," Katz added. The Israeli had worked with most of the intelligence networks of the free world, and he knew how they operated, their strengths and weaknesses. "We ought to get on with this as quickly as possible."

"Well, I set my watch for Washington, D.C. time," McCarter remarked as he glanced at the Le Gran quartz watch on his wrist. "I know it's not 2 a.m. here."

"Thirteen hours' time difference," Said explained. "So it's about 3 p.m. Djakarta time."

"So let's get ready to visit some folks," Manning urged.

"Do we have time to stop by that knife shop, Amir?" Encizo asked hopefully.

"Yeah," James said, "I'd like to get a good blade, too."

"Take them to the shop, and we'll meet you there in ten minutes," Katz said with a sigh. "And make it quick."

"Right," Amir Said assured him. "I just wish I knew where this restaurant was located so I'd have a better idea how far away the shop is."

"We're near Fatahillah Square," Tukarno told him, and rolled his eyes toward the ceiling. "Can't the knives wait?"

"No," Encizo told him, "they can't."

6

Colonel Qui Cham knelt before a small altar and lowered his head in prayer. Smoke rose from incense burners. A bowl of rice, some fish and a small cup of wine were offered to the Buddha. Qui had been raised in the religion, although he did not actively practice it. Long ago he had embraced the creed of communism and the prophets Marx, Lenin and Ho Chi Minh. Yet he still found comfort in the rituals of Buddhism when faced with situations not covered in the teachings of the workers' revolution and socialist doctrines.

Mourning slain comrades was better accomplished by prayers and symbolic sacrifice than simply listing their names as martyrs to a struggle even Hanoi and Moscow no longer seemed willing to fight for. Qui Cham had not forgotten those who had died in the secret war that his superiors had once praised but now denied ever being part of.

Qui recalled the parades of victory when he returned to Hanoi as a hero in the North Vietnamese Army. After the Americans had withdrawn from Vietnam, the ARVN forces of the South were no match for the NVA. The Communist troops took control of the country, winning victories from Laos to Cambodia. The "people's revolution" was winning.

There were plans to continue the expansion of communism into Thailand, Malaysia and Indonesia. After being promoted to full colonel as a reward for his dedication, Qui was placed in charge of a unit of special agents trained to infiltrate these Southeast Asian nations by first infiltrating the groups of non-Communist refugees trying to flee the Socialist Republic of Vietnam. It was a dangerous operation. The refugees hated the Communists and would have torn the agents apart with their bare hands if they suspected they were spies from Hanoi. Qui took great pride in his men and the courage this mission required.

The men had been carefully selected. Each man chosen to infiltrate Malaysia and Indonesia had to be of ethnic Chinese descent. They were required to speak Chinese or Malay and to be able to impersonate merchants, farmers and members of other non-threatening occupations. Qui and forty-two comrades joined the boat people in 1978 and left Vietnam in flimsy little vessels headed for Malaysia.

The journey across the South China Sea was difficult and terrifying. The fragile boats were overcrowded and carried barely enough supplies for their passengers. Heavy seas threatened to capsize the little boats, water splashing into the little crafts in the heavy seas. Various passengers took turns to bail out the steady flow of seawater from their boat. Qui and his men had not been prepared for such an ordeal. They had assumed the boat people were cowardly traitors who chose to abandon their country rather than stay and rebuild it. They had believed such people were weaklings who had grown soft under the corruption of Western capitalist influence.

Yet these people were risking their lives to flee Vietnam. As a Communist, Qui did not understand why anyone would be so desperate to leave the "workers' paradise" promised by the new regime. He wasn't sure if they were very brave or very foolish. The boat people spoke of finding freedom, and they condemned communism for denying them individual rights and private property. What did they know of freedom? Did they have freedom and rights under Diem? Qui believed a Communist government would look after and manage their lives far better than they could do on their own. Qui did not understand why so many would run away.

After several days the passengers were relieved to sight the northeast coast of Malaysia. The long and terrible ordeal was almost finished. Then several police patrol boats appeared, cutting easily through the water, thanks to motor power the Vietnamese crafts lacked. The patrols slowed as they neared the refugees, and the police issued orders in Malay and Chinese through bullhorns. Many of the Vietnamese did not understand either language. Those who did were stunned by what they heard.

The police were ordering them to turn back. Other refugees had fled to Malaysia and had certainly been allowed to land. The Vietnamese knew they could not survive a return trip across the South China Sea. Their supplies were almost gone already.

The refugees continued on to shore. The police motor boats drew closer, and uniformed figures threatened them with guns. The police might as well have threatened to throw rice at them. Whether they died at sea or from a bullet made little difference to the refugees. Malaysia was their only hope of survival.

The police tagged alongside the Vietnamese vessels and continued to order them away from shore. When they were convinced the refugees would not obey, they moved grimly about their business. They hurled grappling hooks that snared the small crafts at stem or stern and, turning the motor boats back out to sea, they towed the refugees away from shore. The Vietnamese screamed and begged the police to have mercy on them. Some tried to dislodge the hooks, but the pull of the motor boats was too strong; the cables attached to the hooks were steel, and the refugees could not cut the lines.

When the police were satisfied that their cargo were far enough from shore, they released them. Some of the boats had been damaged by the operation, and others were weighted down by water from the rough tow and by the struggling passengers. Boats capsized. The desperate people swam to other vessels in hope of rescue, but all the boats were hopelessly overcrowded. Their efforts to board other craft turned over more boats. Qui's own vessel was one of those tipped over by a dozen panicking people.

Qui hit the water. It was warm and salty, but the colonel could swim, and he kept his wits as he clung to the capsized boat. He heard the screams of terror and cries for help from other men, women and children thrashing about in the water. The scene was more terrible than any battlefield Qui had seen.

It was hard to say how long the ordeal lasted. As the long hours passed, the sounds of agony did not cease. Qui and more than a dozen refugees clung to the overturned boat as the tide pulled them southeast and farther from land. They drifted for a day and a night and well into the next day before coming aground on an island in the Malay Archipelago. Only half survived the journey.

An Indonesian fishing boat found them, and the Vietnamese were brought to Java. Qui was separated from his men and had no idea how many of them had survived. He later learned that the Malaysian authorities had banned the landing of Vietnamese boat people in November of 1978 because many of the refugees were ethnic Chinese. The Chinese population in Malaysia had caused problems for the government in the past. In the 1960s, riots had erupted when many claimed the Chinese and Indians controlled an unfair amount of the country's wealth. Under pressure the government decided to prevent a repeat of such problems by denying the boat people permission to land on their shores at all.

The incident in which Qui was involved was one of many, and the Malaysian government reversed the ban after the press reported that several hundred refugees had drowned when the police towed their boats away from the shore. Qui suspected that estimate was rather conservative. He would not have been surprised to learn more than a hundred people had died on the single morning alone when the police hauled his and the other boats out to sea. What disturbed him most of all, however, was the fact that he didn't know if any of his comrades had survived. He had to assume he was the only surviving agent aboard those vessels.

Qui remained in Indonesia and assumed a new identity as a Malay-Chinese. Since he spoke English and French, as well as Malay, Qui soon found employment in the shops that catered to foreigners. He spent the rest of his time learning Bahasa Indonesian and trying to construct an intelligence operation on his own.

He eventually purchased an international transceiver radio and rowed to one of the more than seven hundred uninhabited islands in Indonesia to contact Hanoi and try to find out his own status. He could not reach headquarters, but he did reach a listening post in Ho Chi Minh City. The radio man who received the call didn't understand Qui's coded message, but recognized that it concerned a covert military operation of some sort. He promised to contact his superiors.

The following day Qui called the post again. Someone, apparently an intelligence officer, instructed him to discontinue his broadcast: "You should return to your rice fields and leave the radio alone." In other words Qui was to forget about the mission and return to Vietnam.

Forget about the mission? After his comrades had given their lives for it? What about the great and glorious revolution? Had Hanoi lost interest in the socialist workers? In the years that followed, Qui saw that Hanoi did not seem to want to expand communism across Southeast Asia. The new Secretary General in the Soviet Union spoke of reforms and changes. He wanted greater cooperation with the West, and he actually criticized Vietnam's actions in Cambodia.

Accordingly the leaders of Vietnam and the U.S.S.R. had lost their stomach for the fight. They seemed more concerned with economics and establishing new trade agreements with non-Communist countries than with continuing the struggle for world socialism. Their revolutionary zeal had given in to greed.

Qui was outraged. His family had been killed when the Americans had bombed North Vietnam. Men under his command had given their lives during the war, and his own brave colleagues had died off the coast of Malaysia, only to be forgotten by the government that had sent them. It seemed that only Qui cared about the cause to which he had devoted his life. The politicians may have thought the war over and the revolution ended, but Qui could not accept it.

Qui honored the dead in his own way. He prayed that they would find peace in nirvana, or at least be reincarnated into a world ruled by a single, true Communist state. A world where all would work equally and share equally and no one would want for anything because all were equal. It was a world that would never exist, and Qui realized this, but he still clung to the ideological dream of socialism because the alternative, reality, was an economic and sociological disaster he was unwilling to face.

His parents had raised him as a Mahayana Buddhist. This religion differs significantly from the Hinayana form, which closely follows the original teachings of Buddha, who did not teach of a personal god. Qui's Mahayana beliefs were polytheistic, and he prayed to his chosen gods of war that he would have the strength, courage and wisdom to defeat his enemies.

A RAPPING OF KNUCKLES at the door drew his attention from his altar. Qui rose and pulled back the bolt. The Djarios brothers stood in the corridor and bowed to him politely. The Vietnamese colonel invited them in.

Hasan and Munap entered the room. A small desk faced the door, and a cot was set in one corner, with the altar in another. What few clothes and personal items the colonel owned were stored in a trunk at the foot of the cot. A small wood-burning stove was used to boil water and cook meals. Qui regarded materialism as a crime against everything he believed in. Whatever else one might accuse him of being, Colonel Qui Cham was not a hypocrite.

"Congratulations," Qui announced. "News of your attack on the refinery has reached the news service. It was on the radio an hour ago."

"We lost two good men," Hasan said. "Otherwise, it was a complete success."

He noticed the smell of burning incense and glanced at the altar. Hasan and his brother had been raised as Muslims, although neither had practiced the Islamic religion since they had found the new faith of Marxism. Even so, Hasan tended to regard other religions with disdain. At least the Christians and the Jews believed in some of the same prophets that Muslims do. Adam, Abraham, Moses, Noah and many other figures in the Bible are also in the Koran. Hasan tended to regard Buddhists, Hindus and other religious followers as primitive idol-worshippers. Qui's Buddhism made him uncomfortable.

"It is unfortunate any of our comrades must die," Qui agreed with a sigh. "Of course, such things happen in war. We knew the refinery would be more dangerous than anything *Mérah Tentera* has attempted since I've joined you as assistant commander."

Hasan smiled. He looked at the Vietnamese officer. A small, slender man with a moon face that seemed out of proportion to the rest of his body, Qui did not look like a veteran combat soldier. In his orange robe and sandals, he looked even more harmless, but Hasan knew Qui carried some weapons under his garment. The colonel was never unarmed.

Qui was also being modest about his status as assistant commander. *Mérah Tentera* had been disorganized and undisciplined before the Vietnamese agent had joined their ranks. The others still considered Hasan their commander in the field, but the Djarios brothers knew who was really in charge. They could not argue with results; the Red Army had been far more effective since Qui had taken charge.

The colonel glanced at Munap's right arm. The big Indonesian's sleeves were rolled up, and the tattoo of a red-and-black kris knife was displayed on Munap's brawny forearm. Qui frowned.

"Did you make certain your sleeves covered that?" Qui asked mildly. "If it was visible during the raid on the refinery, an eyewitness might remember it. Tattoos and scars are the sort of things that assist the authorities in identification. Since you got that tattoo while you were in prison, it'll be on your police record."

"They don't keep records of dead men," Munap said with a grin.

"Don't be so certain your files are closed," Qui retorted. "Underestimating the other side is one of the biggest mistakes we can make."

"Munap's sleeves were down during the oil refinery operation," Hasan assured the colonel. "We all wore tape over our fingertips to avoid leaving prints, and we made sure there were no surveillance cameras. We took all the precautions you warned us about, Colonel."

"Baik," Colonel Qui said firmly. "The attack on the refinery will hit the Americans where they are most vulnerable. Capitalists value profit above all else. When the Americans discover it is too dangerous to carry on the petroleum business in Indonesia, they will lose interest in supporting your country."

"I still question the need to kill those two American photographers," Munap commented, his face screwed into an expression of disgust. He did not mind fighting opponents in combat, but killing unarmed individuals was another matter.

"It was necessary," Qui insisted. "The anti-American demonstrations will discourage American tourists with romantic notions of visiting Bali from coming to Indonesia, and will certainly cause some problems with your country's relations with the United States. The Americans will complain to your president that he must maintain law and order to make the country safe for Americans. But that's not enough."

Qui moved to his desk and sat on the edge of it as he smiled at the Djarios brothers. "Do you recall what Lenin said about 'the object of terror'?"

"'The object of terror is terror,'" Hasan replied.

"Exactly. It also stands to reason that the object of terrorism is to create terror. We had to give the Americans and the U.S. government reason to feel terror. Demonstrations would make them nervous, but not terrify them. The idea that any American, even an innocent photographer, could be a victim of terrorism in a place as obscure as the jungles of Borneo will give them reason to fear. Sending the heads to the U.S. Embassy made it absolutely clear that the deaths were political, and it served as a warning to the American government itself."

"You said we can't afford to underestimate our enemies," Hasan commented. "We can't underestimate the Americans, either. They may not be as quick to cut off relations with Indonesia as you seem to believe, Colonel."

"I didn't say it would be quick," Qui insisted. "They might have the CIA poke about and try to bully your government. So what? The Central Intelligence Agency of the United States hasn't been very successful against terrorism in the past. They rely too much on machines. Computers, spy satellites, fancy equipment. Technical intelligence. They think it is superior to 'human intelligence methods.' That's why they are inefficient against terrorism and they won't be any more successful against us."

"We're guerrillas, not terrorists," Munap stated. He did not like Qui's implication that their organization fit the latter category.

"Guerrilla, terrorist, freedom fighter," Qui remarked with a sigh. "The terms are used for the same people by different sides in a conflict. We regard the Contras in Central America as terrorists. The United States consider them freedom fighters. Let's say we're guerrillas using terror to accomplish our goals. My point is the CIA won't get anywhere with us because we're not using so-called high-tech machines and we're not part of any intelligence network they're familiar with. We have more to worry about from the police, especially the Police Mobile Brigade."

"We know all about them, Colonel," Hasan assured him. "Until you joined us, they had all but put our Red Army out of action."

"Within a year they'll be too busy dealing with the riots of the angry masses in the streets to even remember us," Qui announced with satisfaction. "After the Americans leave, as they did in Vietnam, the Indonesian government will not be able to manage this country. The Partai Komunis Indonesia will rise up from the ashes. With the old Communist Party of Indonesia revived, the government will respond as it did when Sukarno ruled."

"That bastard," Munap hissed. "May Sukarno suffer in hell forever for what he did to us."

The parents of the Djarios brothers had been killed by government troops in 1964 when Sukarno was in power.

"I know the idea of such heavy-handed fascism is disturbing," Qui said gently, "but it will work in our favor. Just as Sukarno was forced out of office for his excessive behavior, we will take control with the support of the people behind us. Without the Americans to meddle in Southeast Asian politics, nothing will stop us. Then we'll eventually move into Malaysia and continue the revolution."

"Why Malaysia?" Hasan asked. "The Philippines already has a large Communist resistance movement. The revolutionary zeal in the Philippines seemed to end after Marcos fled, but Corazon Aquino has disappointed many. Since she took control, the economy has slipped and public services have become less efficient."

"Malaysia is closer," Qui said quietly. "And they deserve a revolution. They deserve a very bloody revolution. We'll see to it they get what they deserve."

7

Sumatra stretches over an area of approximately 433,000 square kilometers and extends farther west than the other islands of Indonesia. The Strait of Malacca separates it from the Malay Peninsula. The passengers in the plane gazed down at the dense forest of banyan, palm and rubber trees. It was hard to imagine that more than twenty-eight million people lived on an island that appeared to be mostly jungle.

Rengat is a small city located more than four hundred kilometers north of Palembang, the largest city in Sumatra. The plane landed at a small airfield near Rengat. Yakov Katzenelenbogen, David McCarter, Rafael Encizo, Amir Said and Major Tukarno emerged from the aircraft. The other two Phoenix Force members had remained in Java to check with the last known employer of Sejech Hitam.

Half a dozen soldiers met them at the airfield. Tukarno was in full PMB uniform, complete with field-grade rank and side arm holstered on his hip. The soldiers snapped to attention as he approached. The three Phoenix warriors and Amir Said were dressed in baggy bush trousers with numerous pockets, khaki shirts and boots. They also wore pistols in shoulder holsters and carried backpacks with Heckler & Koch MP-5 subguns with their other equipment.

Encizo had bought two knives at the shop in Djakarta. He carried a Muela Bowie in a belt sheath. It was a big knife made of Spanish steel with a twenty-two-centimeter blade. The other knife was also a Muela Bowie, but considerably smaller with an eleven-centimeter blade with a spear-point tip. It was actually a double-edged dagger, and Encizo carried the smaller knife in a boot sheath—the same way he usually carried his more familiar Gerber Mark I. Both knives had pakkawood handles with brass hand-guards and pommels.

Tukarno had radioed ahead for the soldiers to meet them at the airfield. They had brought two jeeps and a deuce-and-a-half truck. Malay is more widely spoken in Sumatra than Indonesian, and all the soldiers understood the language and some spoke Chinese or Hindi, as well. The major spoke briefly with a lieutenant and turned to Phoenix Force.

"We're ready to go to the plantation," Tukarno explained. "These people might get suspicious if they see Occidentals, so I suggest you three ride in the back. Amir can help me question the employers and co-workers who may have known this Yusaf Kampur character."

"Okay," Katz agreed. "Concentrate on the co-workers. They're more apt to know the sort of details we're looking for. They're probably not involved with the terrorists, so go easy on them. People are more apt to tell the truth if they're not frightened. A scared man will be more likely to tell you simply what he thinks you want to hear."

"And these fellows will probably be nervous when a bunch of military police start questioning them," McCarter added. "That's a natural response. Don't read too much into it."

"I've got a good idea what you want," Said assured the three Phoenix commandos. "Don't worry about it."

"Worrying is part of our job," Encizo remarked. "Sometimes I'm more concerned about getting an ulcer than stopping a bullet!"

"Well, if you get an ulcer, a bullet will probably take care of it," McCarter said cheerfully.

"You're so helpful," the Cuban muttered as he climbed into the back of the truck.

Their trip to the rubber plantation was similar to their ride through Djakarta from the airport. They saw little from the canvas-covered rear of the vehicle. The smell of the rain forest permeated the heavy air. The rich fragrance of flowers and the stench of decaying vegetable and animal matter smelled to them like being near a garden and a compost heap at the same time. Despite its pungency, the jungle's earthy, natural organic odor smelled not at all like the choking fumes of factory waste and human-generated garbage that one encounters in the cities.

Hundreds of sounds reverberated in the rain forest around the truck. Exotic birds called and monkeys chattered. They heard something like a bestial roar, but this could have been an engine of one of the vehicles and not the sound of a great jungle cat. Tigers are still found in Sumatra, although their numbers are decreasing as man continues to consume their natural environment for his own use.

Eventually the sounds changed, and they heard the voices of men and the growling of machinery. The truck came to a halt. The three Phoenix commandos peered through a space between the canvas tarp and the wooden ribs attached to the overhead beam. They saw a forest of thick, dark trees and men dressed in lightweight work clothes and conical hats of woven rice reeds. It was the rubber plantation.

"We'll be waiting here for a while," Katz commented. He leaned back on the bench and sighed. "May as well try to get comfortable."

"I bloody hate this part of the job," McCarter complained as he got out his Player's and fired up a cigarette.

Encizo tried to wave the smoke away from his face. He was a nonsmoker and he hated being in an enclosed area with someone puffing cigarettes. Katz closed his eyes and bowed his head. The Israeli had learned that it was best to take advantage of any opportunity to rest during a mission. He allowed himself to drift into the shallow, first level of sleep as the minutes crawled by.

Nearly two hours passed before Amir Said pulled back the tarp and climbed inside. Katz raised his head and instinctively reached for the Beretta M-92 under his right armpit as he was abruptly roused. He recognized Said and moved his hand away from the butt of the pistol.

"Are you all right?" Said inquired.

"I'm fine," Katz assured him. "What did you learn?"

"Yusaf Kampur wasn't a very popular man," Said answered. "He kept to himself, didn't talk much to his co-workers and basically did his job and kept away from the others as best he could. They all knew he'd been in prison, but they didn't know why he had been in Ek Penjara or that his crimes had been connected with politics. He didn't talk much about politics except for an occasional grumble about the government. Of course, everybody complains about their government."

"Everybody has reason to," Encizo replied. "Doesn't sound like this trip accomplished much."

"The major is talking to management, and I don't think he'll have any success at all," Said continued, "but I did learn one thing about the late Mr. Kampur. One worker remembers seeing Kampur with some tough-looking characters at a village about fifty kilometers east of here. He said Kampur left with them in a beat-up old truck. When he asked the villagers who those men were, they warned him to keep away from those guys.''

"Did they say why?" McCarter asked, finally interested in the conversation.

"They said they were hoodlums of some sort," the ex-CIA agent said. "Probably hill bandits, or at least that's what the villagers thought. They said these roughnecks have a camp up at the foot of the Barisans. That would mean they'd have to be at the mountains nearest the center of Sumatra. I doubt the villagers would know if they were located along the west coast.''

"How many are there?" Katz inquired.

"The man I talked to said Kampur was with five other men," Said answered. "The villagers didn't give any number, but we'd better assume there are more than five.''

"It could be a local base for the terrorists," Encizo remarked as he checked a map. "The oil refinery was on the east coast in Sumatra. The terrorists could have their base of operations at the mountains and send scouts ahead to recon the plant and steal the telephone company truck at Djambi or one of the other cities in the area.''

"That would be one hell of a break if we nail these blokes this easy," McCarter mused. "What do you think, Mr. Colby?"

Katz blinked and remembered "Colby" was his current cover name. He took out a pack of Camels and thoughtfully considered the situation.

"It'll be dark soon," he began. "We'll have enough trouble finding the camp...if indeed there really *is* a camp. It would be even more difficult at night. There are two things we should try to do first. Let's contact Miller and Jones and have them meet us at Rengat. We also need to learn some more information about this alleged hoodlum camp before we make our next move.''

''I just hope this doesn't turn out to be a blind alley,'' Encizo remarked glumly as he waved more cigarette smoke away from his face.

''There's only one way to find out,'' the Phoenix commander said.

GARY MANNING AND CALVIN JAMES arrived after dusk on another plane with Sergeant Jatta. They had looked into the commercial fishing boat owned by Chin Ho Li in Java to question the man about Sejech Hitam, the other terrorist killed during the raid on the oil refinery. They had drawn a blank. Chin and his entire crew had gone down in his vessel somewhere in the Indian Ocean nine months ago with no sign of any survivors.

Phoenix Force and their Indonesian allies gathered together at a restaurant in Rengat. The waiters were excited when the senior military officer and five foreigners entered the restaurant. Sumatra is usually overlooked by tourists and the waiters hoped the visitors would spend a lot of money there. The manager himself came forward to welcome them in broken English and escort them to a large table.

The manager suggested they have *rijsttafel*, a classic traditional Indonesian dish. Tukarno and Said explained that the waiters would bring several dishes to accompany great portions of boiled rice or *nasi*. These would vary from bananas and pineapples to chicken and beef. *Rijsttafel* used to consist of more than forty selections, but now it usually includes a maximum of five. The manager assured them that his cooks could provide at least ten selections. He even had one non-Muslim cook who could prepare *babi panggang* barbecued pork. Swine flesh is forbidden in Islam. The same is true of alcohol, but the manager informed them he had some beer in stock. He apologized that he did not have any gin.

"The British and the Dutch generally have gin as a before-dinner drink with *rijsttafel*," Said explained. "While you fellows are in Indonesia, you really should enjoy the *rijsttafel* as a major dining experience."

"I agree," Tukarno added. "I also suggest we have them prepare extra *bakso udang goréng*. They're shrimp balls and really quite delicious."

"Shrimp balls—" James began with a grin.

"Don't say it," Katz interrupted. "The meal sounds excellent even if I mispronounce it. We'll pass on the beer, however. It's important we all keep clear heads."

"I don't suppose they have Coca-Cola?" McCarter asked, prepared to be disappointed.

Said checked with the manager and discovered the Briton's favorite soft drink was not available. Both coffee and tea would be served with the meal. McCarter reluctantly accepted his fate. The manager and the waiters left them to see to the meal.

"Something else we found out before we left Djakarta," Manning began. "Your computer whiz, Sergeant Mudo, plugged into a U.S. Embassy computer and discovered another package has arrived. This one contained a human hand instead of heads. It hasn't been identified yet, but I don't think it takes any great powers of deduction to figure out it's probably the hand the terrorist cut off Peter Waldo at the refinery."

"These sons of bitches send some sick calling cards," James remarked. "Whoever they are, it seems pretty obvious they're trying to frighten Americans away from Indonesia. Those here on business, as well as those connected with the U.S. government."

"The attack on the refinery suggests there's a good chance the terrorists didn't know the American photographers they killed in Borneo were actually NSA agents," Katz remarked.

The men at the tables were silent as waiters arrived with coffee, tea, rice and the first offerings for *rijsttafel*. Although none of the waiters appeared to understand English, Phoenix Force and their companions did not resume their conversation until the waiters had left.

"You figure we can establish contact with NSA and CIA?" Said inquired. "We can use all the help we can get."

"Not yet," Katz answered. "I think we should be at least eighty percent positive the American intelligence networks are secure before we bring them into it."

"Why only eighty percent?" Tukarno inquired.

"Because one hundred percent security doesn't apply to CIA or NSA anymore," Katz explained. "In the good old days of espionage, the main concern were sleeper agents and moles in your organization. Now the chance of someone selling out his country for financial gain is as great as being violated by enemy agents."

"Not to mention traitors like Kim Philby," McCarter added. "Did you know that bastard had the nerve to write a book called *My Silent War* that explained why he betrayed British intelligence and went over to the Russians?"

"Philby died a couple years ago," Manning said. "We don't have to worry about him anymore."

"So he's dead?" McCarter said with a shrug. "I'm still mad at him anyway."

"That's awfully useful information," James snorted. "What I'm really curious about is this mysterious camp up in the mountains and whether or not these dudes who hung out with Kampur are terrorists or just some run-of-the-mill lowlife.''

''I told Lieutenant Hidjah to investigate those claims,'' Major Tukarno explained. ''He's the executive officer in charge of the men who met us at the airfield. Hidjah and his soldiers know Sumatra better than any of us, and they can get information from the locals much faster than we can. He's already headed for the village where Kampur allegedly met with the so-called bandits. If the people there support this story, he'll spend the rest of the night checking villages and towns near the Barisan mountains where that camp is supposed to be.''

''Speaking of camps,'' Katz began, ''we ought to find a place to get some sleep tonight and be ready to leave if your lieutenant succeeds.''

''I suggest we head out of town,'' Tukarno stated. ''We can set up some tents and get some decent sleep and maintain radio contact with Hidjah in case he tries to call us. Besides, I think you'll find Rengat doesn't have much to offer as far as hotels are concerned.''

No one could argue with that. The city consisted mostly of wooden shacks and dirt roads. There seemed to be a few cars or trucks in the entire town, although some young men with bicycle-powered rickshas had offered to give them a tour of Rengat for five hundred rupiahs, less than one American dollar.

''We'll take your suggestion, Major,'' Katz said. The waiters returned with more trays of food. ''You were certainly right about the *rijsttafel*.''

''You pronounced it right, Mr. Colby,'' Said declared.

''My first victory in Indonesia,'' Katz remarked. ''I hope it won't be the only one.''

8

A radio message came from Lieutenant Hidjah a few minutes after 2 a.m. He had discovered similar stories about a hoodlum camp from other villages near the Barisan mountains. He told Major Tukarno to meet his group outside Muarabungo, which is located near the center of Sumatra.

Tukarno roused Phoenix Force and the others. They struck camp and headed for Muarabungo. The roads were poorly kept, and the ride was rocky and uncomfortable. However, there was virtually no other traffic, and they made reasonably good time. Once the vehicles came to a halt when some tapirs blocked their path. Large nocturnal ungulate mammals, tapirs look like huge pigs with modified donkey ears and abbreviated elephant trunks. Actually the animal is more closely related to the rhinoceros than any of the animals it resembles. The beast has remained almost unchanged since its ancestors appeared during the Pliocene period. The tapirs ignored the headlights, but they squealed and galloped for a nearby lake when the drivers honked their horns at them.

They drove on to Muarabungo and met Lt. Hidjah and his men at the outskirts of town. The junior officer had learned that some of the villagers had seen the campfires of the group who had supposedly been involved with Kampur only two weeks ago. They also thought that the mysterious outfit was still stationed at the base of one of the mountains. A local Batak villager was willing to guide them to the camp for seven thousand rupiahs. Phoenix Force was more than willing to accept the offer.

The journey had to be made on foot through dense foliage in the predawn darkness. With no roads they used parang machetes to cut their way through thick vines and enormous ferns. Insects, tree frogs and night birds paused in their singing as the men approached, resuming their night sounds as the human intruders moved on.

At last they saw the peaks of the Barisans in the distance. The sky glowed golden with daybreak. The moon was visible above the slanted top of the nearest mountain. The volcanic mountains extend across Sumatra in several bands, most dramatically near the west coast, where Mount Kerinci, the largest of the mountains, is found.

Manning raised his G-3 rifle and peered through the Bushnell scope mounted to the frame. He trained it on a small blaze at the base of the nearest mountain. Several tents surrounded the campfire beside which a weary-looking figure squatted on a rock, a British Lee Enfield Mark V cradled in his arms. Large boxes covered with canvas tarps were half-hidden in the shadows behind the tents.

The Canadian described what he saw to the others. All the men were armed either with an assault rifle or a submachine gun. Katz and Amir Said took command of half the team, with Said in charge of the non-English-speaking soldiers. Major Tukarno, Encizo and McCarter commanded most of the others, but Manning, James and Sergeant Jatta formed their own division within the group.

Since the men at the camp had their backs to the wall of the mountain, Phoenix Force and their allies only needed to cover three angles to box in the so-called hoodlums. The leaders of each section of the team reminded everyone to hold his fire and not to jump to conclusions. They could not be sure who or what the men at the camp might be. Perhaps they were surveyors with a mining operation, or simply a group of hikers who liked some genuine challenge for adventure. The sentry's rifle did not mean anything in particular. It was not uncommon for people to be armed in the Sumatra rain forests.

Phoenix Force and the others formed themselves into a horseshoe to surround the camp on all sides. The foliage was thinner and offered scant cover as they neared the base of the mountain, but they used the tall elephant grass, massive ferns and other vegetation as much as they could to conceal their movements.

Katz gestured with his hooks to signal when they were in position. He braced the H&K subgun across his prosthesis as Said nodded and signaled to his troops, as well. The Phoenix commander had complete faith in his fellow Force members to judge the right spot to bring their parts of the unit to a halt. Indeed, the voice of Major Tukarno soon shouted out orders in Indonesian to warn the camp that they were surrounded and to throw out their weapons or the Police Mobile Brigade would be forced to open fire.

The sentry leaped up with a startled expression on his face. He threw himself behind the rock he had been sitting on and braced the Lee Enfield across the stone. Lieutenant Hidjah began to repeat Tukarno's instructions in Malay in case the men in the camp did not understand Indonesian. He was still bellowing orders when two of the tents collapsed and men appeared at the camp with weapons in hand. Most carried British rifles similar to the sentry's, but one held an old Thompson submachine gun, and another wielded a long bolt-action rifle.

Manning had already trained his G-3 at the man who had ducked behind the rock. The sentry presented the smallest target and had the best cover, which made him the most potentially dangerous for the moment. The Canadian marksman lined up the cross hairs of the Bushnell scope and fixed the center on the man's forehead above the rock. He squeezed the trigger and blasted a single 7.62 mm slug through his skull. The bullet tunneled a path through the gunman's brain and smashed open the back of his head in a fraction of a second.

The guy with the Thompson swung his chattergun at the area from which Lt. Hidjah had spoken. Katz fired first and nailed the man in the chest with a trio of 9 mm Heckler & Koch messengers. The man triggered his Thompson as he fell and sprayed one of the tents with a volley of .45-caliber rounds. Bullet holes appeared in canvas, and more men scrambled into view, including one unfortunate fellow clutching a fresh wound in his side.

Several opponents dived for cover by some boulders while others opened fire without bothering to aim, hoping to convince Phoenix Force and their allies to stay low and hold their fire. Calvin James hissed an obscenity as a stray bullet tore into a fern beside his left arm. The slug burrowed into the ground harmlessly near his thigh.

"You shouldn't have scared me," James rasped as he pointed his M-16 at the camp and raised the barrel. "I get pissed off when I'm scared."

He triggered the M-203 grenade launcher attached to the underside of the barrel. A 40 mm grenade belched from the big barrel, sailing high above the camp and into the mountain. It exploded on impact, disloding large chunks of rock that showered down on the camp.

Figures tumbled from behind the boulders. The remaining tents collapsed under the small avalanche. Some furious and desperate opponents charged forward, weapons held ready. Rafael Encizo aimed low with his H&K MP-5 and sprayed a salvo of 9 mm rounds at the legs of a pair of advancing gunmen. They screamed and toppled to the ground, their thigh bones splintered and kneecaps shattered. One man passed out, but the other crawled on his belly and tried to point his revolver at Encizo's position.

The Cuban triggered the H&K once more and blasted the man's skull with a trio of parabellums. The gunman sprawled on the ground, never to move again.

One of the soldiers made the mistake of standing up to get a better view of the camp while trying to pick a target among the enemy. The triggerman armed with the bolt-action rifle promptly aimed and fired. The Indonesian trooper cried out as he fell.

McCarter saw the soldier go down and swung his Heckler & Koch chattergun at the trooper's killer. The Briton triggered the submachine gun and raised it slightly, moving with the climb of the barrel. A trio of 9 mm rounds cut a lethal swath straight up the rifleman's chest from his solar plexus to the top of his sternum. The rifle fell from his grasp as he stumbled back several steps and dropped lifeless to the ground.

More charging opponents fell to the gunfire of Tukarno and the other soldiers. A couple of gunmen rushed to the large canvas-covered boxes. Phoenix Force and the others in the raiding party were reluctant to fire on them because they didn't know what was concealed beneath the tarps. Half a ton of explosives could have been hidden under the canvas. Dynamite or some other explosives would be easily detonated by a bullet, killing everyone in the camp and possibly some of the assault team, as well.

"Worry them," Katz told Said. "Get their attention for a second or two."

He demonstrated what he meant by firing his H&K chopper. Bullets plowed into the ground near the covered packages. Said followed his example by aiming high with his MP-5 and spraying a burst of 9 mm slugs into the rock wall above the boxes.

A gunman soon thrust the barrel of his Lee Enfield from cover to fire at Katz and Said. The pair took cover as bullets hammered a large log in front of them. Their opponent leaned forward to get a better aim. Gary Manning had him in his sights and fired his G-3, a 7.62 mm slug shattering the gunman's left elbow. the British rifle whirled and spun from his fingers like a baton.

McCarter boldly charged from cover and advanced on two other men using the second tarp-covered box for shelter. He fired his MP-5 low to try to scare them out. Two rounds spit from the muzzle, and the H&K clicked on empty. He cursed under his breath as he saw the two turn their guns in his direction. McCarter dropped the subgun and dived to the ground, his hand streaking for the Browning under his arm.

One gunman's head suddenly recoiled as three 5.56 mm slugs plowed through it. Calvin James had moved to a new position and trained his M-16 on the enemies that threatened his British teammate. The slain opponent fell against the second man, who was trying to point a side-by-side shotgun at McCarter. The guy nearly lost his balance and held his fire a moment too long.

McCarter had drawn his Browning and gripped it in both hands as he snap-aimed and triggered two shots. One 9 mm parabellum smashed into the upper lip of the man with the shotgun and shattered his top row of front teeth.

The other slug tore into the bridge of the guy's nose and into his brain.

Several dead and wounded opponents littered the ground. Only two had escaped uninjured. They threw their weapons down and surrendered, pleading in Indonesian, Malay and a couple of local dialects. One even gave himself up in English. Phoenix Force and the soldiers ordered the survivors to raise their hands and slowly advanced toward the camp.

Encizo approached a still form on the ground and prepared to kick the man's rifle beyond his reach in case he was still alive. Suddenly the guy's Enfield rose in a high arc. The buttstock struck Encizo's H&K subgun and knocked the weapon from his hands. The man rose on unsteady legs, his face contorted by pain and rage. A ribbon of blood oozed from his open mouth, but the fury in his eyes announced he still had enough fight to try to take Encizo with him as he died.

As he reached for the handle of the Muela Bowie in his belt sheath, the Cuban grabbed the frame of the opponent's rifle to hold the weapon at bay. His knife hand lunged and drove almost half of the twenty-two centimeters of Rockwell 56-58 steel into the man's stomach. With grit teeth Encizo dragged the blade upward from the man's solar plexus. His opponent howled in agony until the blood gurgled from his mouth in globs of crimson. Encizo felt it spill hot across his fist and wrist, and then his opponent sagged against the knife blade. He actually felt the man die before he turned the Muela and yanked out the steel.

"You all right, mate?" McCarter inquired with concern when when he saw the blood on the Cuban's clothing.

"Just a little messy right now," Encizo assured him.

Tukarno and Said ordered the remaining defenders to face the mountain and to keep their hands in clear view. Soldiers frisked them and confiscated their weapons before handcuffing them. Manning walked to the fallen bolt-action rifle and picked it up. He frowned as he examined it.

"A Swedish Model 40," the Canadian announced. "Eight millimeter. It's been obsolete for the last forty years."

"Their weapons haven't been used in regular military service anywhere in the world for decades," Katz agreed as he glanced down at a discarded Enfield rifle. "I guess most of these weapons are World War II vintage. They've probably been shuffled from owner to owner ever since the Japanese occupied Indonesia in the 1940s."

"Is this important?" Tukarno inquired as he approached the Israeli.

"The terrorists at the refinery were armed with modern firearms," Katz explained. "M-16 rifles, Beretta M-12 submachine guns and other up-to-date firearms, as well as weapons used with *pentjak-silat* martial arts. These guys aren't armed with anything like that."

McCarter walked to one of the canvas-covered boxes and yanked off the tarp. Inside the large cage's iron bars sat a black ape with extremely long arms and a small torso. He jumped about in terror and clung to the top bars with long strong fingers.

"What the hell is this?" the Briton exclaimed with surprise.

"It's a siamang," Amir Said explained. "A black gibbon. A rare species of ape found only in Sumatra. They're protected from hunters and trappers by law."

McCarter pulled away the second tarp and revealed another cage with a larger, reddish-brown ape inside. It looked up sheepishly from a heavy brow ridge and smacked its wide mouth nervuosly. Said told the Briton the second primate was an orangutan.

"Yeah," McCarter muttered. "I recognize this one. What are these bastards doing with these beasties?"

"Believe it or not," Said said, "there's an illegal black market for rare animals. Some circuses and small zoos would pay thousands of dollars for either one of these apes. There are even a few rich members of the Arab royal families and some Third World dictators who love to spend money on everything but their people and would probably pay a million bucks just to have one of these fellows in a private menagerie."

"You mean we bagged a bunch of poachers?" James said with a groan.

"Actually we killed most of them," McCarter commented.

"Don't remind me," the black commando muttered.

"They started shooting and they didn't give us much choice," Katz stated. "These fellows weren't exactly innocent bystanders."

The gibbon chattered and shook its cage while the orangutan uttered some grunting sounds that seemed to express sorrow. McCarter turned to look at them. Incredibly neither animal had been harmed during the battle. They only looked frightened of what would happen next.

"You two blokes take it easy," the Briton told them. "You're the only ones to come out ahead on this deal. You get to go home, but we're right back where we bloody started."

9

Amir Said and Major Tukarno interrogated the two remaining poachers. Lieutenant Hidjah assisted with his command of the Malay tongue in the area. When they finally reported their findings to Phoenix Force, the news was not as pessimistic as McCarter had voiced to the two caged primates.

"These trash remembered Yusaf Kampur," Tukarno announced. "They say he joined them in their loathsome black-market business. Not surprising that scum like this often sat about a campfire and drank alcohol like the heretics they are."

Major Tukarno was a devout Muslim. Then he realized his comments might offend any member of Phoenix Force who drank spirits and apologized for his remarks.

"That's all right, Major," Katz assured him. "None of us are that thin-skinned. Did Kampur ever say anything after he'd had a few drinks? Men have a tendency to speak rather freely when they're bending the elbow with their companions."

"That's the best news of all," Said answered. "Little Yusaf apparently ran off his mouth a lot when he was drunk. He may have kept quiet around his co-workers back at the rubber plantation, but he talked plenty to his poacher pals. He bragged about being a freedom fighter...excuse the term...with the *Mérah Tentera*. He boasted that he knew the Djarios brothers personally, and they were going to lead the Red Army in the revolution to liberate the working masses and all that Marxist dribble."

"The Djarios brothers?" Katz said thoughtfully. "Does that mean anything to either of you?"

"The name sounds vaguely familiar," Tukarno stated, "but it is not an uncommon name in Indonesia. Sergeant Mudo may be able to help us identify them when we get back to Djakarta. Let's hope they managed to find a place somewhere in his computer sources."

"I'm a U.S. citizen now," Said commented. "Remember? Don't expect me to know too much. But I may be able to pick up some bits and pieces of information by contacting some people I know."

Calvin James shuffled forward, a grim expression on his ebony features. The Phoenix Force medic had been busy treating the wounded, including the poachers who had been injured during the battle.

"One of Lieutenant Hidjah's men is dead," James announced. "Two others were wounded. One's a flesh wound, but the other has a smashed shoulder joint. We need to get them both to a hospital. No bullet wound is ever anything less than serious."

"We'll get them out of here as soon as possible," Katz promised.

"I've already got some stretchers being made," James stated. When he treated injured men, the commando did not wait for permission to do what needed to be done to save their lives. "Some of the poachers have to be carried out of here, too. I don't want any of the soldiers taking out their frustrations on wounded men because they're mad these dudes killed one of their own and tagged a couple others with slugs. They want to kick somebody's ass, but they can wait until the sucker heals first."

"They'll also have to wait for this human garbage to get out of prison," Tukarno added. "The government of Indonesia takes such crimes very seriously."

"The poachers also told us where they captured the siamang and the orangutan," Said stated. "We'll pass the area on the way back to the trucks. The primates should be released in the immediate area they're familiar with."

"I'd rather help the apes than the goddamn poachers," McCarter muttered sourly.

"You can probably relate to them better," Manning replied.

"How droll," the Briton growled. "The poachers were shooting at us. The gibbon and the orangutan weren't."

"Gee, you notice everything," the Canadian said sarcastically. "I guess we won't have to give the apes paraffin tests to find out if they fired any guns recently 'cause you noticed they didn't take part in the shootout."

McCarter was about to respond to Manning's barbs when James cut him off before he could begin.

"This ain't the time for your Abbot-and-Costello routine," James said sharply. "We have wounded men who need more medical care than I can give 'em, and that ain't bullshit."

"That's just what I was about to say," McCarter declared, and snorted at the Canadian.

"I'd say we all have a lot of work to do," Katz added.

THEY RELEASED THE PRIMATES in the appropriate areas of the rain forest. The apes eagerly headed for the trees and disappeared in the foliage. The group continued to drag improvised litters with the wounded until they cleared the jungle and reached the trucks. The injured were gently placed inside the vehicles. Guards stayed with the wounded poachers, and the other prisoners were handcuffed once more before the trucks rolled on to Muarabungo.

While Major Tukarno and Lt. Hidjah gave a partial explanation of what had happened to hospital administrators, the wounded were treated in the emergency department. Sergeant Jatta called Mudo at the safehouse in Djakarta and instructed him to check out the Djarios brothers. By noon Phoenix Force, Tukarno, Said and Jatta were once again headed for Java by plane.

Tukarno suggested they have lunch when they arrived at Djakarta before returning to the safehouse. This allowed Phoenix Force their first good look at the capital of Indonesia by light of day. The sight was sadly disappointing. Most of the population of more than seven million seemed to live in rundown shacks that made American slums look like high-quality housing by comparison.

Modern structures of steel and glass stood side by side with shabby wooden dwellings. Canals extended through parts of the city, evidence of Indonesia's Dutch influence. However, Djakarta is not Amsterdam, and the hot humid climate made the canals stagnant and ideal breeding grounds for insects and disease.

Although the canals served a questionable purpose, Indonesians were definitely mobile in the streets of Djakarta. The traffic was as hectic and unruly as anything Phoenix Force had seen in the streets of New York or Rome. Cars, trucks and buses competed with motor scooters, bicycle-rickshas and odd-looking three-wheeled trucks. Said told the Phoenix members these strange vehicles were called *bemos*. They had seen similar little three-wheelers in Europe, but they had never heard traffic that was as noisy. Everything from foghorn-style bellows to high-pitched whistles filled their ears. If there were any rules to driving in Djkarta, no one seemed to pay much attention to them.

They steered clear of the Pasar Ikan. This was the major fish market, and it was packed with people who seemed ready to kill each other over the choicest seafood on sale. The restaurant Tukarno recommended for lunch was some distance from the markets. On the way, they glimpsed the stunning alabaster dome of a beautiful mosque in the distance. Said explained that this was on the grounds of the presidential palace.

The restaurant manager recognized Major Tukarno and cheerfully greeted him and his guests. The officer clearly enjoyed his opportunity to display Muslim hospitality. He was trying to extend the motto "all that is in my house is yours" to include the entire city of Djakarta, if not his entire country.

Once again Phoenix Force followed the advice of the native Indonesians. Tukarno insisted that *bifstik Djawa* was a special Javanese delight and suggested *sate* appetizers and *lumpia goréng*. None of Phoenix Force had any idea what these dishes were, but they were not disappointed by the major's selection. The appetizers were small cubes of beef and chicken, and the *lumpia goréng* proved to be similar to a Chinese egg roll filled with shrimp and beef. The main course was a fine steak dinner prepared with spices and tenderizers. The house blend Java coffee and the *pisang goréng*, banana fritters, rounded out a superb meal.

"Most of the time during a mission we usually eat stale sandwiches and C-rations," James said with a contented sigh.

"Two meals in restaurants in less than twenty-four hours," Encizo added with a grin. "I think that's a first for us."

"They didn't have any Coca-Cola," McCarter muttered miserably.

"It was another fine meal," Katz assured the major, "but we should be getting to the safe house, now. Sergeant Mudo has been slaving over a hot computer, and I want to know if he's found some information about the Djarios brothers."

MUDO DID NOT DISAPPOINT them. He had printout sheets on Hasan and Munap Djarios waiting for Phoenix Force and the others when they returned. Tukarno translated the information for his comrades.

"These two first came to the attention of the authorities when they assaulted a shop owner when they were seventeen and fifteen," Tukarno explained. "The court went a bit easy on them because they were orphans and had been living on the street since their parents were killed."

"How were they killed?" Manning inquired.

"Victims of Sukarno's administration," the major said grimly, "or at least associated with his regime. You fellows in America may not remember much about Sukarno. He was president in the 1950s and established what he called a 'Guided Democracy' with himself in charge as the guide. He virtually set himself up as the one-man ruler of Indonesia. At this time, the communists—known as the PKI, or Partai Komunis Indonesia—stepped up its antigovernment activities and the army retaliated with a heavy hand."

"And the United States was supporting Sukarno and was associated with his actions," Encizo said with a grunt. "This sounds familiar."

"Wait a second," Said began. "Uncle Sam *didn't* approve of Sukarno. CIA and Taiwan intelligence covertly assisted an anti-Sukarno rebel movement from 1956 to 1958. However, by then it was too late, and the rebels were no match for the army."

"But the United States was associated with Sukarno when he adopted an anti-Communist stance," Tukarno insisted. "Washington may not have liked Sukarno, but they obviously liked the idea of a Communist takeover in Indonesia even less. There were house-to-house searches, arrests and trials with questionable evidence and a number of murders that were probably by death squads. Anyone opposed to Sukarno or who even criticized him was apt to be labeled as a member of the PKI."

"There was a snowball effect from this," Said added. "Sukarno actually tried to modify his policies to bring an end to the mess, but certain army factions and some of the more militant Muslim groups didn't want to stop. Anyone they didn't like, they accused of being PKI members. This even continued when General Suharto took over in 1966. Oddly enough Suharto had been the military strategic commander under Sukarno and, the year before, he had saved Sukarno's tail by suppressing a coup attempt by other military dissidents who, among other things, assassinated six of Sukarno's top generals. Then Suharto himself took over by using less bloody methods."

"Suharto was an improvement?" James asked.

"Most Indonesians would agree with that," Tukarno said. "Not that there haven't been complaints about human rights violations under him, as well. Hundreds of thousands were arrested and accused of being involved in the attempted coup in 1965, and they were sent to prison. Less than a thousand of these people ever stood trial. Some of them remained in prison until 1979. The PKI was outlawed, and the Communists weren't too happy about that. Every national election there are clashes between extremist groups and the military. That's to be expected, I suppose."

"There are actually a number of countries where that doesn't happen," Said remarked. "That's one reason I'm a U.S. citizen now."

Tukarno stared hard at Said. Katz reminded the major they needed to know more information about the Djarios brothers specifically.

"They served less than two years in a juvenile correctional institution," the major replied as he checked the printout sheet. "They were allowed to serve time together because they were very close after having only each other to rely on for so long. However, shortly after they were released, they were arrested for taking part in a violent antigovernment demonstration. There wasn't any proof they actually harmed anyone, though, so they were lucky enough to get one year each in Ek Penjara."

"The same prison Kampur and Hitam stayed in," Encizo remarked. "Interesting."

"It gets more interesting," Sergeant Mudo commented. He already knew what was on the fact sheet and waited for Tukarno to get to the best part.

"Hasan and Munap Djarios seemed to have wandered about from job to job for a while before they found employment with—" Tukarno raised his eyebrows "—Chin Ho Li."

"The same commercial fisherman who hired Hitam," Manning recalled. "The fellow we couldn't talk to because he was lost at sea."

"According to this the Djarios brothers were aboard the vessel when it went down," Tukarno announced. "Wreckage was found of the boat, but no bodies. That's not surprising because there are sharks in the Indian

Ocean. The Djarios brothers and everyone on Chin's boat are officially listed as dead.''

"Sounds like Chin made some bad choices of crew mates," Said commented. "The Djarios must have sunk the vessel, probably killed Chin, and used the incident as a way to disappear so they could work with the *Mérah Tentera* without having to worry about parole officers looking over their shoulders.''

"What else do we have on them?" Katz inquired.

"Physical descriptions," Tukarno answered with a shrug. "The most useful item is that Munap has the tattoo of a kris knife on his forearm, and he's bigger than the average Indonesian. Nothing else about either man would stand out in a crowd.''

"Well," McCarter said with a sigh. "Now we have an idea who we're after, but we don't know where the hell they are. I'm going to get a Coke.''

One of three phones on Tukarno's desk rang. The major picked up the wrong receiver on the first grab, but found the right phone the second time. He looked grim when he hung up.

"A demonstration was just started in front of the U.S. Embassy," the major announced. "Apparently they're blaming the deaths of Indonesian civilians at the oil refinery on the American company that owned it and the U.S. government. That didn't take long to get organized.''

"No, it didn't," Katz said thoughtfully. "In fact, there may be a reason for it happening so soon. *Mérah Tentera* themselves may have organized it for their own purposes.''

"You mean this could be another terrorist strike?" Sergeant Jatta asked with alarm.

"It's possible," the Israeli replied. "Maybe it's paranoia on my part, but I'd rather check into it than do nothing and have the terrorists carry out a hit while we're back here.''

"No rest for the weary," Manning said with a groan. "We'd better move."

10

The protesters formed a ring around the front of the U.S. Embassy. They waved signs written in Indonesian and English that denounced American involvement in Indonesia and accused the petroleum companies of murder. A few signs were less dramatic and simply complained that U.S. oil refineries were more concerned about the safety of their derricks than their workers.

Military police armed with automatic rifles, batons and side arms divided the protesters and the Embassy. They wore helmets with *Polisi* printed above the brim and kept the crowd at bay by sheer intimidation. How long that would be enough was hard to say. The demonstrators were young and angry. Some carried rocks and bottles. At least none of them had gas bombs or Molotov cocktails, although it would not be difficult to make them by siphoning some gas from a parked car and sticking a rag in the mouth of a bottle and lighting it.

The situation was very tense when Phoenix Force, Tukarno, Said and Jatta arrived. The PMB major and his aide marched to some military vehicles near the protest and discussed the matter with the riot control officers. Phoenix Force had donned civilian jackets and windbreakers to conceal their shoulder holsters and pistols. Calvin James and Rafael Encizo joined Tukarno at the front of the Embassy. Since Indonesians tend to think of Americans as white and Aryan in appearance, the black and Hispanic commandos were less apt to draw attention from the unruly crowd.

The other three Phoenix members and Said covered the rear of the Embassy. Gary Manning raised his Bushnell binoculars and scanned the crowd and surrounding area for any sign of danger. The Canadian stayed behind the cover of a car, a straw hat pulled low on his brow to help conceal his Caucasian features. Katz carried a two-way radio, as well as an overnight bag with an MP-5 hidden inside. McCarter accompanied the Israeli as they moved along a sidewalk behind the Embassy. The Briton held a video camera to his shoulder and peered through the lens to scan the area.

Two hostile youths marched toward the three Phoenix pros and Amir Said. They snarled "Yankees!" and some other expressions in their native language. Said stepped forward and assured the angry young men that his companions were with a French news service and not Americans.

"Que veut dire ceci?" Katz demanded as he stared at the youths. *"Je ne comprends pas."*

The pair seemed disappointed and turned away to rejoin the demonstration at the front of the building. Said looked at Katz and sighed with relief. The ex-CIA man stepped closer and whispered to the Phoenix commander.

"What if they wanted more proof?" he inquired.

"Miller and Collins speak French, too," Katz assured him, using Manning and McCarter's cover names. "That's why we picked this disguise."

"That's great for you three," Said commented, "but I don't speak French, and it would be sort of hard to explain why I was with you guys as a translator or guide."

"Just pretend to understand and say *oui* a couple of times if any of us say anything in French," Katz told him. "Then turn away from us as if you're annoyed at having to put up with us. We're just trying to fool people in passing, not trying to pass a language course."

Suddenly a burst of automatic fire erupted. Screams from the mob announced the demonstrators had been the targets. Manning spotted a muzzle-flash and swung his binoculars toward it. The Canadian saw a rifle barrel withdrawn into a fifty-story window about half a block away.

"Got him!" Manning announced as he yanked open a car door and reached inside for his G-3 rifle. "Redbrick building! The tall one halfway down the street! Sniper is upstairs!"

"Let's nail the bastard!" McCarter exclaimed as he bolted toward the site.

Said ran after the British ace while Katz grabbed the radio on his belt and reported the information to Major Tukarno. Manning gathered up his assault rifle and headed for the building. McCarter and Said had already reached the door.

THE DEMONSTRATION HAD instantly become a riot after two protesters fell to the ground, blood streaming from bullet wounds. The mob did not consider where the shots had come from. They automatically assumed the attack had been carried out by the military police or the U.S. Embassy or perhaps both working in conspiracy together.

"Holy shit!" James exclaimed as a dozen screaming young demonstrators charged toward him and his Cuban partner.

"How are you at bowling?" Encizo asked through clenched teeth. He rushed to a wooden blockade as he spoke.

James hurried to the opposite end of the two-meter-long, sawhorse-style barrier. Encizo grabbed his end and raised the wooden legs. James nodded and followed his example. They heaved the barrier at the advancing crowd, throwing it low at their legs. The long center beam chopped into the knees and shins of four furious members at the front of the mob. They cried out and fell to the pavement. Others tripped over their fallen comrades and tumbled beside them.

Another protester used the fallen shapes as a springboard to launch himself at James and Encizo. He screamed in rage and wielded a short stick in his fist as he landed in front of the Phoenix pair. James stepped back as if recoiling and suddenly whirled on one foot to lash out a tae-kwon-do wheel-kick. The back of his heel slammed hard into the man's abdomen, and he doubled up with a surprised gasp.

Encizo quickly stepped forward and drove a hard uppercut under the youth's jaw. The punch sent him hurtling backward into more charging figures. Another protester weaved around his stumbling companions to swing his picket sign at James's head. The tough commando from Chicago dodged the attack. The sign swooped past James and struck the pavement near his feet.

James grabbed the shaft of it between the attacker's fists to pin down the pole long enough to keep the guy from trying another swing while James delivered a short, hard punch to the youth's chin. The fellow's head bounced, and he started to lose his grip on the pole. James's roundhouse kick under his ribs threw him off balance. The demonstrator's fingers slipped from the shaft of the picket sign, but James managed to hang on to it.

A skinny young protester attacked Encizo and swung a wild flailing punch at the Cuban. Encizo ducked low and moved forward to grab the arm behind the lunging fist. He hauled his attacker over his right shoulder and straightened his knees as he bent forward. The kid hurled head over heels over the Phoenix pro's shoulder and crashed to the pavement.

A pair of hands grabbed Encizo from behind. He immediately drove an elbow back into the new opponent and was rewarded with a breathless groan. The Cuban glanced over his shoulder at the youthful face an instant before he delivered another elbow stroke to the guy's mouth. The second attacker fell senseless to the ground while the fellow Encizo had tossed with a judo throw started to get up. The Cuban warrior stepped closer, stomped a boot near the opponent to distract him and swung a hard left hook to the side of the youth's jaw. He too dropped unconscious at his feet.

James swung the confiscated protest sign at two more opponents and drove them backward. One tripped over a fallen comrade. The other was distracted when he saw his pal topple. James took advantage of his diverted attention to quickly thrust the end of the pole into the fellow's gut. The youth doubled up with a gasp, and James snap-kicked him in the face to drop him like a stone.

"I hate it when this happens," James rasped as he chased off another opponent simply by threatening him with the picket sign. "Riot control ain't our job, damn it!"

The military police had clashed with the other demonstrators. Rifle butts and batons struck down several young zealots. Protesters hurled rocks and bottles. One cop screamed and staggered away, his face badly cut by broken glass. Protest signs swung at helmeted heads. Police fell in battle, but more of the untrained and unprotected protesters dropped as the battle continued.

When the police became more concerned about their own survival, guns were fired. More bodies fell and panicked protesters started to flee. Cops chased them and brought them down with baton blows and rifle butt-strokes. Major Tukarno yelled something at the other military cops. Almost as an afterthought, when it served little purpose, tear-gas grenades were lobbed at what remained of the angry crowd.

James and Encizo watched the police club and kick fallen opponents into submission. Tukarno was clearly furious with the officers in charge of riot control, but they did not seem to think their men had done anything wrong. Broken figures lay sprawled in the street on spreading crimson stains on the pavement, the number of dead and injured far exceeding the number still left on the ground.

"I told them not to shoot!" Tukarno exclaimed angrily as he approached James and Encizo. "I told them the real enemy is a block away!"

"When all hell breaks loose, you can't expect anybody to pay much attention to reason," James remarked. His nose twitched as the wind blew tear-gas fumes in their direction.

Gunfire continued from the direction where Katz had reported the sniper. The Phoenix pair remembered their three partners were still in trouble and bolted toward the sound.

DAVID McCARTER and Amir Said had reached the tall redbrick building a few minutes earlier. They heard the bedlam in progress at the front of the Embassy and knew the demonstrators and police had clashed. For the moment all they could do was try to get the persons responsible for triggering the riot in the first place.

The Briton jogged into an alley and gestured for Said to head inside the building. Whoever did the shooting would not calmly wait for them in the room upstairs. The bastard—or, more likely, bastards—would try to get out of the building as fast as possible. McCarter would cover the outside, while Said entered the building. They knew Katz and Manning would soon follow to back them up, so neither man would be on his own for more than a couple of seconds.

A chattering of automatic fire suddenly forced Said to dash into the alley behind McCarter. Bullets tore at the edge of the bricks at the front of the building. Said yanked his Browning from his shoulder leather and he flattened his back against the wall. He glanced at McCarter, who was holding his Pindad Hi-Power in his fist.

"The sniper has backup," Said explained, gasping for breath from the tension rather than any physical effort. "They fired from the other side of the street."

Gary Manning and Yakov Katzenelenbogen headed for the building and saw the gunmen shoot from the cover of a *bemo* three-wheeled truck parked on the curb. One man leaned around the nose of the vehicle with a Beretta M-12 subgun to fire at the fleeing figure of Amir Said. At least one other gunman was behind the *bemo*. His head and the barrel of his assault rifle were visible above the roof of the odd little truck.

An unlucky rider on a motor scooter also arrived and lost control of his bike when the terrorists triggered another salvo of machine gun fire. The rider swerved and crashed into a trash barrel at the curb. He fell, hitting the pavement hard. A truck behind the scooter came to an abrupt halt when the driver saw what was going on. Another car behind the big truck was unable to stop in time, and it slammed into the rear of the larger vehicle.

The sudden end of traffic flow on the street kept innocent people out of the line of fire as Manning raised his G-3 rifle and quickly moved to a lamppost. The Canadian marksman dropped to one knee and aimed as carefully as the urgency of the situation allowed. The gunman with the Beretta chopper glanced about and saw Manning. A stocky man clad in gray coveralls and a black knit hat, he swung his M-12 toward the Canadian's position.

The Canadian triggered his H&K assault rifle and blasted a 7.62 mm round into the upper chest of the terrorist. The impact of the bullet drove the gunman backward as he triggered his Beretta and fired a 3-round burst of 9 mm slugs into the frame of the *bemo*. Manning fired his G-3 again and drilled his opponent once more in the chest, just left of center. The terrorist went down from the 7.62 mm "heart attack."

The rifleman behind the three-wheel truck aimed his M-16 around the rear of the *bemo*. He had forgotten about McCarter and Said. The latter pointed his Browning at the enemy rifleman and triggered two shots. One parabellum smashed a side window of the *bemo*, and the other struck the vehicle's frame near the terrorist's left arm.

"I missed him!" Said rasped with disgust as he ducked back around the corner. "I should have spent more time at the firing range after I left the Company!"

McCarter did not argue with him. The Briton glanced down the opposite end of the valley. A Dumpster and two trash cans blocked part of his view but he could see that the alley extended to the rear of the building.

"Stay here and help keep them busy," McCarter said. "Keep an eye on the alley, too. I'm going around back to make sure the snipers don't escape that way...."

He stopped in midsentence when a figure emerged from a second-story window. A lanky man with long legs and arms swung down from the windowsill and jumped to the lid of the Dumpster. He landed on his feet, hands raised as if to surrender, although he carried a pistol jammed in his belt.

"Henti!" Said ordered, and pointed his Browning at the man. The order was hardly necessary, because the guy did not seem to be going anywhere.

McCarter hardly glanced at the man, but kept his eyes trained on the windows above. A rifle barrel poked over the sill of the same window the guy had jumped from. McCarter raised his Browning and fired two rounds at it. The M-16 rifle slid from the sill and fell on the Dumpster near the startled man who still stood on the lid.

"I'm impressed, Collins," Said told him as he approached the Dumpster, pistol trained on the remaining opponent. "How did you guess there was another one up there?"

"The sniper used a rifle, and this bloke isn't carrying one," McCarter answered, and moved to the edge of the building to help draw the attention of the other opponents still facing his fellow Phoenix warriors. "If this fella really intended to surrender, he probably would have tossed out his pistol first. I just figured he was supposed to distract us and gambled we wouldn't shoot him because he pretended to give up. That meant there was probably another bastard waiting to get the drop on us."

Said instructed the man on the Dumpster to use two fingers of one hand to slowly remove the pistol from his belt. The guy obeyed, gingerly holding the handgun between thumb and forefinger. He tossed it into a garbage can and hopped down from the Dumpster. He grunted as he landed against the trash bin, as if he had turned his ankle.

In a flash he grabbed the M-16's barrel on top of the Dumpster and swung the rifle at Said. The ex-CIA man ducked. He continued to hold his fire, reluctant to shoot a man who would be more valuable alive than dead. The terrorist took advantage of his hesitation to deliver a quick kick to his wrist, knocking the Browning from Said's hand.

McCarter turned and saw the terrorist slash a cross-body chop at Said's throat. The ex-agent's forearms swung forward to bat the attacking arm aside. Said rapped the knuckles of the back of one fist into his opponent's face and turned to drive an elbow into the man's ribs. The terrorist groaned and dropped to the ground.

He had not been knocked down by the blow. In a flash the terrorist displayed his own knowledge of *pentjak-silat* by lashing a leg into Said's ankles. The stroke swept Said off his feet, and the terrorist sprang forward and he drew a short-bladed dagger from a boot sheath. McCarter swung his pistol at the opponent, but Said had already reached up and grabbed the man's wrist above the knife.

Said braced himself on his back and shoulders as he thrust a foot into his opponent's armpit. The terrorist gasped as the blow to the nerve center under his arm stunned him. Said held on to the wrist and forearm in a grip like steel as he rolled to one side, his foot still planted under the other man's arm. The terrorist was thrown off balance and hurled to the ground. Said shifted his body, pivoting on the small of his back, and held on to his opponent's knife hand as he moved his foot from the guy's armpit to slam his heel into the side of his head. Said kicked him once again, and the terrorist slumped unconscious at last.

McCarter grunted with approval, relieved that Said was all right and pleased by how the former CIA agent had handled himself. Then he returned his attention to the street as the terrorist by the *bemo* truck exchanged shots with Manning once again.

THE CANADIAN DUCKED LOW as bullets whined off the lamppost. He took comfort in the knowledge that Katz had circled around the truck and the car stopped in the middle of the street. The Israeli used the vehicles to conceal him as he crept steadily across the street. Katz held his MP-5 ready.

The terrorist's attention was divided between Manning and the alley where he knew another opponent was stationed. He did not notice Katz until the Israeli closed in on him. Startled, the gunman swung his M-16 in the Phoenix commander's direction.

Katz fired the Heckler and Koch submarine gun. A trio of 9 mm parabellums crashed into the terrorist's chest above the breastbone and through the throat. The impact threw the man back onto the pavement, blood spewing from his gouged throat. He still clutched the M-16 by the pistol grip in one fist and tried to raise the barrel. Katz stepped foward and stamped a boot down on the rifle. The weakening terrorist knew there was nothing more he could do.

He gazed up at Katz, defeat in his eyes. It was the last thing he felt before he died. Katz kicked the rifle from his fingers and signaled to Manning that he was safe. The Canadian stepped from behind the lamppost and saw James and Encizo coming their way.

"Everybody okay?" James asked eagerly.

"I think so," Manning said with a nod. "How did it go with the demonstration?"

"Not too good," Encizo replied, "but it could have been worse. It's bad enough. At least four people were killed. Maybe more."

"Well, the sons of bitches responsible didn't get away," McCarter announced as he stepped from the alley. "Amir managed to take one of them alive. I shot one through the window. We'd better find him, but I don't think he's going anywhere."

"I just hope we're goin' somewhere with this," James muttered. "I guess I shouldn't be too disappointed. We did second-guess the terrorists and we finally caught up with some of them."

"Yeah," Encizo added. "The trouble is the terrorists accomplished most of what they intended to do. They didn't really lose this round, so we didn't really win, either."

"It's not over yet," Manning assured him. "Not even close."

11

"The sniper shooting succeeded in causing a riot," Hasan told Colonel Qui, "but the sniper and backup personnel did not get away. Only the men assigned to the trucks a quarter of a kilometer away managed to escape."

Qui Cham listened grimly to the report. He avoided looking at Hasan and Munap Djarios in the face. Instead, the Vietnamese colonel stared at the top of his desk until he was certain he could conceal the surprise and anger he felt.

"The riot was violent enough to cause the police to fire some shots," Hasan continued. "It might have been bloodier if two men at the front of the Embassy hadn't been there. They brought down about a dozen protesters without firing a shot. The drivers of the escape trucks watched from the rooftops with telescopes. They said the two foreigners were truly impressive."

"Foreigners?" Qui asked with interest. "What kind of foreigners? Americans?"

"The observers weren't sure," Hasan answered. "One was a tall man. Very dark. They described him as an African. The other was shorter and muscular. His complexion could have been Southeast Asian, but they said his features were different, perhaps Mediterranean."

"There are many African-Americans and Spanish-Americans," Qui remarked thoughtfully. "Many of the latter also have West Indian blood, so they tend to be darker than the European Spaniards. What happened to the attack team and backup?"

"Four men were stationed at the rear of the Embassy," Hasan replied. "The moment shots were fired, they raced to the building. They were armed and very skilled fighters."

"So they anticipated we might strike during the demonstration," Qui remarked with a frown. "They even had some idea what sort of tactics we might use."

"How could they?" Munap asked. "Who would 'they' be? If the CIA did this, they would have had more people involved. Yet at least three of the men at the rear of the Embassy were supposedly foreigners. Caucasians. One was even supposed to be a gray-haired man with an artificial arm...."

"A prosthesis?" Qui asked sharply. "Were the observers sure about this?"

"When they first noticed the three white men with what appeared to be a tour guide, they dismissed the group as harmless because one of the men was middle-aged with an artificial arm," Hasan admitted.

"A foolish assumption," Qui snapped as he suddenly rose from his chair and started to pace the floor. "I once had the privilege of serving under General Ton Chi Dai. He lost his hand during the war and had a steel hook at the end of his arm. General Ton was still a fine soldier and a superb fighting man."

Hasan remembered reading about Ton in the newspapers a year ago. The Vietnamese general had stolen a vast fortune in gold and precious gems from temples in Cambodia to finance a scheme to purchase nuclear cannons from an American arms dealer named Heller. It had been a major news story all over the world for almost a week.

Hasan had admired General Ton's spirit and determination, but he believed Ton had failed because he had made the mistake of trusting an American gangster.

"I also recall reading rather sketchy intelligence reports through KGB sources when I was still in Vietnam," Qui continued. "There were occasional stories of a one-armed agent and commando who worked with various intelligence networks of the West. Supposedly he speaks several languages fluently so no one can be certain of his nationality. If even half of these reports applied to the same man, this one-armed mystery man has a career that rivals that of Sidney Reilly at the turn of the century."

"You think this could be the same man?" Hasan inquired. "Is he working with CIA?"

"I haven't been in contact with Hanoi for over a decade," the colonel said, "but I have established nongovernmental intelligence sources with arms dealers, black marketeers, various types of informers in Southeast Asia. Rumors about an elite five-man commando unit have persisted since the mid-1980s. Apparently they work for the Americans and their leader is a one-armed middle-aged man. The other four members fit the descriptions you gave of the individuals responsible for ruining our operation at the U.S. Embassy."

"Ruined is too strong a term, Colonel," Hasan insisted. "The strike succeeded in its original goal."

"But four of our comrades did not escape," Qui retorted. "We have to assume at least one was taken alive, and he'll be forced to reveal more information about us. He may even tell them where this base is located."

"None of our men will talk," Munap declared proudly. "Even if they torture our comrades, they would sooner die than betray us."

"That's unrealistic, Munap," Qui told him. "Any man will break if the right methods are used. Torture isn't necessary, and I doubt professionals would use it. I've been present when prisoners were tortured for information. They'll talk after a while, but they'll tell the torturers whatever they think will work to get the pain to stop. There are more reliable methods, such as truth serums or simply forcing a suspect to go without sleep long enough. The Russians discovered this can break down a man's resistance to interrogation as early as World War I, and it's been a favorite method with them ever since."

"But that could take days," Hasan stated. "Certainly more than forty-eight hours."

"Not with the assistance of certain drugs to increase the process," Qui insisted. "The Soviets have used certain sulfur compounds for treatment in institutions to correct the mental attitudes of political dissidents. They also learned these injections could break down a subject's will in a manner similar to sleep deprivation. This can cause brain damage, of course, but I myself wouldn't hesitate to use such methods to get information. We must assume the enemy will have no qualms about doing it, either."

"I don't understand why we should be concerned about a small five-man commando team," Munap declared. "What can they do if CIA and the PMB have been powerless against us?"

"A small group of men can often accomplish what entire armies cannot," Qui answered. "Castro started the Cuban revolution with only ten trained men. During the Vietnam War, the Viet Cong were often more effective in small bands than the NVA in major military operations. Likewise, the American Special Forces and similar groups often worked better against us than massive attacks by regular military. When we fought tribes of the Montagnards, we learned that a few, highly skilled warriors—even armed with primitive weapons—could be a match for large army units with modern firearms and artillery."

"*Mérah Tentera* itself consists of only a hundred and eleven men in total," Hasan added. "I agree with you, Colonel. This could be a very serious threat to us."

"Let them come to us," Munap said, a fist clenched in rage. "We'll crush them in open battle. I'll willingly face any one of them in hand-to-hand combat. I can kill any American pig with my bare hands."

"They couldn't operate effectively in Indonesia if they were working on their own," Qui said with a sigh. He was sometimes annoyed by Munap's thickheadedness. "When they come for us, there will be considerably more than five opponents to deal with."

"To say 'when' they come instead of 'if' they come does sound a bit negative," Hasan observed. "These super-commandos may be good, but they're not infallible."

"No one is," Qui agreed, and stroked his chin thoughtfully. "We need to make some plans in advance. Hasan, I want you to round up approximately one third of our comrades here and get them ready to leave. Don't tell them where they're going, but I want you to have them down at the docks in two hours."

"Do I get to know where we're going?" Hasan asked dryly.

"To our other base in Borneo," Qui answered. "We have a man there named Fong. You know him?"

"A Malay-Chinese," Hasan confirmed. "He's a skilled forger and he's a bit older than most of our comrades."

"I want to see him in my office," Qui said. "I also need two other men, but I'll have to pick them based on physical size and age."

The colonel turned to face Munap. "When you were in Ek Penjara, you gave several fellow prisoners tattoos besides yourself, correct?"

"That's right," Munap confirmed with a smile. "I became quite good with a needle and ink. No one ever complained about my work."

"I hope that I won't have any reason to, either," Qui replied.

AMIR SAID HELPED Calvin James interrogate the lone survivor of the terrorist attack at the U.S. Embassy. He was impressed by the commando's care in administering a precise injection of scopolamine. The Phoenix Force medic had first estimated his subject's weight and physical condition. He had checked heartbeat, blood pressure and even examined a blood sample under a microscope. Only after he completed his tests was he ready to give the prisoner a dose of truth serum.

"Scopolamine is sort of tricky," James told Said. He stood next to the subject and pulled back the man's eyelid as he spoke. "If you don't use enough, it's not effective, and if you use too much, you'll kill your subject."

Said looked down at the limp figure strapped to the armchair. The lanky terrorist sprawled across the chair, seemingly asleep, his head bowed forward. A purple bruise had formed on the side of his face as a mememto of his fight with Said in the alley.

"Have you done this before?" Said inquired with some concern.

"Lots of times," James assured him. "About forty times over the years. It usually works. Once in a while you come across a real frothing-mouth fanatic who won't do anything but rant and rave under the drug's influence. But scopolamine generally works pretty well. It's the only truth serum that's really reliable, and even it isn't perfect.''

"I know," Said replied. "I once saw a man die during interrogation because his heart couldn't handle the drug."

"This son of a bitch is healthy enough. I've never lost a patient during interrogation, and I don't intend to start now. One thing scopolamine doesn't do is give a fella the ability to speak or understand English if he doesn't already know the language. It's best to question the guy in his native tongue."

"I understand," Said replied. "I'll translate your questions into Indonesian and his answers into English."

"Exactly," James confirmed as he checked the guy's pupils again. "Okay. This sucker's ready for question-and-answer time. Get Colby and Tukarno in here. They'll want to be part of this."

Katz and Major Tukarno entered the room. It had formerly been a rest room to the *Penén Rumah* restaurant before the building was converted into a safe house by the Police Mobile Brigade. There were still sinks and toilets in the room. James had strapped the prisoner to an armchair in the center of the room. He wanted a private room where he could run tests without outside noise and distractions. Interrogations were best done without other voices or the traffic sounds interfering with the question-and-answer session. The rest room was the best quarters available under the circumstances.

They began the interrogation with fundamentals. They asked the subject his name, age, nationality and what color his hair was. He replied in a slow, slightly slurred voice. He said his name was Rasul Barinjin, a twenty-five-year-old Indonesian born in the island of Madura. He also claimed his hair was black, the only fact they could confirm at that point.

Barinjin admitted he was a member of *Mérah Tentera* and that he had been sent with three other comrades to fire into the political demonstration in front of the Embassy. The intention had been to start a riot, creating a number of dead martyrs when the police reacted to gunfire with their own weapons.

Tukarno asked a question in Indonesian without going through Said as a translator. Barinjin muttered *"ja"* in reply. The major explained that he had inquired if the terrorists had been acting under orders from the Djarios brothers. Katz urged Tukarno to wait until they asked less pressing questions to give the man time to get used to responding to inquiries under scopolamine's influence.

"Ask him what the Red Army's goals are," Katz said.

The terrorist replied that they intended to foment a people's revolution to overthrow the Golkar-controlled government. After Indonesia was "liberated," their struggle would extend to Malaysia and eventually branch out to other countries in the Pacific.

When asked why the *Mérah Tentera* had targeted Americans in particular, Barinjin explained that the United States had been a longtime supporter of the "imperialist government" in Indonesia. In 1975, Indonesia's financial strength nearly collapsed when Pertamina was unable to repay debts greater than one hundred billion rupiahs.

"What's Pertamina?" Katz asked Tukarno.

"The state-owned oil enterprise in Indonesia. This terrorist slime has his history right. The country was on the verge of an economic collapse in the mid-1970s, but the United States and other Western democracies helped salvage our economy. The increase of American petroleum operations has also been mutually advantageous to both Indonesia and the U.S."

"That certainly explains why they attacked the refinery," Katz mused. "They think if they can drive out American business and U.S. support, Indonesia's economy will collapse and the nation will be ripe for revolution."

"And they're probably right," Said declared. "This country *would* collapse into revolution if the economy fell."

"Just because you decided to leave Indonesia and become an American citizen doesn't give you the right to criticize it at every opportunity," Tukarno suddenly snapped.

"Oh?" Said replied with raised eyebrows. "You mean there hasn't been widespread unrest and open hostility toward the present government in Indonesia in the past? In 1978 there were student demonstrations all over this country. In 1982 there were violent clashes in the streets between Muslim groups and the military during the national elections. That all happened long before *Mérah Tentera* appeared."

"Hey, shut up for now," James told them. "Save the debate until we finish the interrogation."

They asked why the two wildlife photographers were killed. Barinjin only knew that they were picked because they were in Borneo at the right time and the Djarios brothers wanted some dead Americans to send a frightening message to the U.S. Embassy. He was not sure if it was the Djarios brothers' idea or the colonel's.

"Who the hell is the colonel?" James asked.

Said translated the question. Barinjin explained that all he knew about the colonel was that the man was Chinese, probably Malay-Chinese, and that he acted as a strategist and adviser to the Djarioses. The *Mérah Tentera* was very impressed with the colonel.

"That's interesting," Katz remarked. "Where can we find the Djarios brothers and this colonel?"

The prisoner told them about an old temple in northwest Bali that served as the main headquarters for the Red Army. Hasan and Munap were usually at the base, and the colonel was virtually always there. So were the majority of the *Mérah Tentera* members. Usually no fewer than sixty, depending on how many were in the field on recon missions or other assignments.

"Sounds like we hit the jackpot this time," James announced as he checked Barinjin's pulse. "We got a chance to take out the whole organization in one fell swoop."

"We'll also have to take on about sixty or more opponents," Said remarked.

"Well, Major," Katz began as he turned to face Tukarno. "I certainly hope you can get us some more troops on short notice."

"I'll call in as many as possible," Tukarno promised. "I just hope it will be enough."

"We can't use too many men, or we'll never be able to approach the base unnoticed," Katz warned. "They'll certainly have sentries posted, possibly informers in the area, and they may even expect trouble if the colonel assumes we managed to get one of his people to talk."

"You think the colonel is the real leader?" Said asked.

"Judging from the information on the Djarios brothers, I doubt they could have organized a bunch of fellow exconvicts and whoever else is involved in this and gotten this far on their own," Katz answered. "This outfit seems to have some degree of military expertise."

"I'll have Mudo run a computer check on anyone who has used the title 'the colonel' and been involved in terrorist or mercenary activity in Southeast Asia," Tukarno volunteered. "Who knows? He might turn up something.

Meantime, I need some idea how many men we'll need for the assault on that temple."

"Twenty or twenty-five going in," Katz replied. "Perhaps forty or fifty for backup to come in after we penetrate the base and begin dealing with the terrorists from within."

"I don't suppose we could just blow the hell out of the base with artillery," Said remarked with a sigh.

"We might hit the wrong place," Katz answered. "It's possible Barinjin gave us false information even under the influence of scopolamine. We don't want to blow up a temple and find out we killed innocent people. Besides, there are other terrorists running around Indonesia, and it will be easier to round them up if we can get our hands on some records or at least interrogate other *Mérah Tentera* members to get an idea where the rest of their comrades might be."

"So we have to do it the hard way," James said with a shrug. "Nothin' new about that."

12

The island of Bali seemed a most unlikely place for a terrorist group's headquarters. From the Boeing-Vertol CH-47 Chinook helicopters descending at Tuban Airport, the passengers saw the surrounding area seemed green and lush. Palm trees swayed gently in the breeze, and the hills in the distance seemed untouched by modern man. Bali looked like a paradise, and everyone aboard the Chinooks could understand why Indian Prime Minister Jawaharlal Nehru had once referred to the island as "the Morning of the World."

The great choppers were almost obscenely out of place. Long, powerful helicopters with big rotor blades at each end, they resembled giant mechanical dragons invading the Garden of Eden. The majority of aircraft of Tuban were Garuda Indonesian Airways planes bringing tourists, but military aircraft occasionally landed at the port for fuel during maneuvers.

The Chinooks' doors slid open, and uniformed figures emerged. They wore Indonesian army fatigues and carried weapons and backpacks, but their uniforms did not bear the eagle-and-thunderbolt crest of the Police Mobile Brigade, and they wore helmets instead of the dark blue berets of the PMB. The troops walked about and stretched their backs and limbs as if trying to work stiffness from their bodies. More than seventy men stepped from the two

Chinooks, each helicopter large enough to carry a maximum of forty-four.

While some of the troops met with airport personnel to help pump fuel into the massive tanks of the Chinooks, others wandered about the hangars. Some lighted cigarettes and engaged in quiet conversations. The confusion allowed Phoenix Force, Amir Said, Major Tukarno and thirteen other PMB soldiers to wander unnoticed into a hangar. Two three-ton trucks were parked inside. The men climbed into them and covered the rear opening with canvas tarps.

"This cloak-and-dagger business doesn't make things easy," Major Tukarno commented as he sat on a bench next to Katz.

The Israeli removed his helmet and placed it on the floorboards by his feet. "No, it doesn't, but it's a necessary precaution. The terrorists probably set up a base in Bali because they figured no one would guess this would be the site for such a headquarters."

"I certainly wouldn't have guessed there could be anything like that here," the major admitted. "In fact, Bali has been remarkably free of political hostilities. Most of the unrest has been in Java, Sumatra, the Moluccas, the Celebes and, of course, Timor. Bali has been virtually free of such troubles."

"That just means we don't know how long the terrorists have been located here or how large their intelligence network is," Katz insisted. "We have to assume they sent someone to the airport when the Chinooks arrived. Hopefully they'll see the troops return to the aircraft after fueling and depart and be convinced there was nothing unusual about the incident."

"I hope you're right," Tukarno said with a sigh.

"It was the best we could come up with on short notice," Gary Manning remarked as he stretched his legs and glanced at the soldiers with them who had volunteered for the most hazardous part of that night's mission.

They were young and physically fit. Some of them had had previous experience with terrorist groups and revolutionary zealots, but none of them had participated in anything like the current assignment. Some seemed anxious and others were eager. A few looked stoic and kept their emotions concealed behind blank features.

Most carried M-16 assault rifles or Beretta M-12 submachine guns. The officers also had side arms, and nearly all the PMB carried knives. Some carried parang machetes, but the majority favored the traditional kris with a long, wavy double-edged blade.

They waited half an hour after the Chinooks had left with the majority of the troops. At last the trucks rumbled out of the hangars and away from Tuban Airport. They drove past rows of coconut palms on the road to Denpasar, the capital of Bali.

The city did not look like the paradise Bali had seemed to be from the air. The shanties and slums around Denpasar contrasted appallingly to the natural beauty of the island. The population faced starvation when crops failed in a bad year. The residents sat quietly by their ill-made shacks and watched the trucks pass by. Many smiled and waved. A few of the soldiers tossed a few rupiahs to those with their hands out.

In the distance the ten-story high Hotel Bali Beach rose, a proud monument to all the luxury that foreign tourist money could buy. Original construction of the first-class high-rise had begun on the demands of none other than President Sukarno himself. It now had more than five hundred rooms, not including the Bali Seaside Cottages, run by the same management. The Hotel Segara Village is also located in the area. More than in any other province or island of Indonesia, tourism is big business in Bali.

As the trucks rolled through Denpasar, they were forced to stop as a group of dancers swayed through the streets. Several beautiful young women in colorful silk garments carried large jugs of water and plates of food on their heads. The reputation of Balinese women for being among the most beautiful in the world derives in part from the superbly delicate features associated with the Polynesians. The women swayed and sang, their burdens gracefully supported.

The dancers and the crowd were accompanied by the music of drums and bronze gong instruments that sound similar to xylophones. In the midst of the joyous crowd moved several smiling men who carried a litter on their shoulders. The still figure wrapped in white linen on it was decorated with heaps of bright exotic flowers.

"What the hell is this?" James inquired as he peered from the truck's canvas flap to watch the scene. "A festival or a funeral?"

"Both," Amir Said answered. "They're celebrating the cremation of a loved one. All his friends and family are here to see him off."

"You're serious?" James asked with surprise. "They're gonna burn that dude in the sheet and they're having a party over it?"

"Haven't you ever heard of an Irish wake?" McCarter asked with a shrug. "Although this does look a lot more cheerful than any wake I ever saw."

"The Balinese consider death a time to rejoice," Said explained. "They believe a cremation means the loved one's soul has been released from worldly cares and suffering. They don't see anything to be sad about. Somebody they cared for has been liberated to go on to a better life."

"Life back in those shanties must suck," James muttered. "Maybe these folks have a point."

"Islam is the major religion of most of Indonesia," Said stated. "Bali is the exception. The majority of people here are Hindus. Actually it's sort of Hinduism with a lot of Polynesian beliefs mixed in. It's such a unique religion, developed here on the island, that it's officially known as Bali-Hindu."

"It looks like they're having a good time," Rafael Encizo remarked. "I guess a festival is a good way to lift one's spirits when you live in poverty."

"They have festivals here all the time," Said told him with a laugh. "You wouldn't believe it unless you stayed here awhile, but the Balinese celebrate everything from weddings and birthdays to having a dentist clean their teeth and put in some fillings. These are very warm, friendly people. One reason is they've been almost unspoiled by the rest of the world."

As the trucks drove north from Denpasar, Said explained a little more of Bali's history. During the long occupation of the Dutch in Indonesia, Bali was virtually ignored. The Indonesian government had allowed Bali to pretty much handle its own affairs. The island was largely agricultural, raising rice, sugarcane and coffee.

Indeed, the twentieth century seemed to have only a nodding association with Bali. There were practically no factories or mills on the island. There were no freeways, and the roads were little more than dirt paths. It was not the easiest terrain for the trucks as they rattled along their journey from one end of the island to the other. Bali is only a hundred and forty-five kilometers long and ninety kilometers wide, but the poor roads made the trip seem much longer.

The scenery was magnificent. The lush tropical vegetation was everywhere, extending to the terraced hillsides where the rice crops were irrigated. Toward the center of the island, the small convoy approached a chain of mountains. The highest, Mount Agung, was a volcano that last erupted in March of 1963. Clouds of smoke and ash rise from its crater.

The trucks passed through a few small towns and hamlets, where more lovely young ladies appeared. Many of them were naked from the waist up. A few of the Muslim soldiers in the trucks looked away and muttered some sort of complaint or perhaps prayers that Allah would grant them strength. Most of the troops did not object to the sight. And none of Phoenix Force was upset at all.

"I think I could really learn to like Bali," Encizo commented as he smiled and waved at one woman who returned the gesture, unconcerned with the jiggle of her naked bosom.

"The central government at Djakarta issued an order some years ago that no female is permitted to walk about in public without covering her breasts," Said informed his Phoenix companions. "They didn't pay much attention to that rule here in Bali, except in Denpasar."

"I certainly admire these ladies' civil disobedience," James commented.

Twilight was descending as the trucks rumbled northeast. In the distance they saw the city lights of Singaradja, the major port city of the island. Their destination was near the coast, about ten kilometers from Singaradja, where Barinjin had told them the temple was located. A temple that no longer drew worshippers, but was being used by the *Mérah Tentera* for secular and destructive purposes.

What little Phoenix Force had been able to learn about the Temple of Parashurama seemed to support what the prisoner had told them back at the safehouse in Djakarta. Parashurama is an avatar or incarnation of the Hindu deity Vishnu. According to legend, Parashurama decapitated his mother and killed the entire Kshatriya class to avenge his father. Although Hindus tend to take a less literal interpretation of such stories than most Christians or Muslims do the stories of the Bible or the Koran, Parashurama's bloody legend made the temple less than appealing to the peaceful and amiable people of Bali.

The Temple of Parashurama eventually lost all worshippers and remained only as a curiosity. The Balinese, like people everywhere, were reluctant to tear down a place of worship even if it no longer served that function. They had considered the idea of converting the temple into a place of sanctuary for monkeys, similar to the Sacred Forest near Sangeh Temple, where tame monkeys are fed by residents and tourists. However, nothing was done, and the abandoned temple was simply left, perhaps to allow Parashurama to have the place to himself.

Phoenix Force, Amir Said and the Police Mobile Brigade forces left the trucks at the side of a dirt road and made their way through the dense foliage for the last kilometer to the temple on foot. Major Tukarno raised the antenna to a two-way radio and pressed a button twice. A small red light flashed twice in reply.

"We're still in radio contact with Captain Mendang," Tukarno announced as he put the radio away.

Mendang was the officer in charge of the troops staying with the two Chinooks. They would be called in for reinforcements and air support when needed. Katz nodded.

There was nothing more to say to the other Phoenix commandos and their allies. They knew what to do and they were ready to begin.

THEY BRANCHED OUT in two groups. Katz, Manning, James and Major Tukarno led one group, while McCarter, Encizo and Amir Said commanded the others. Silently they stalked the Temple of Parashurama. A full moon amply lighted the area, so the men did not require night-vision gear. They had to be cautious because the bright moonlight would also reveal them more readily to their enemies.

They worked their way through the high elephant grass and thick clusters of ferns until they were about two hundred meters away. Sleek domes with short spires stood above the gray stone walls. Sculptures of Hindu deities and avatars crowded the facade of the building. Once brightly painted in many colors, the statues were faded and dull in the cool moonlight. The largest figure was a man-shape wearing ornate headgear and bracelets at the wrists and ankles. The double-edged battle-ax in one fist identified the statue as Parashurama, the incarnation of Vishnu meaning "Rama-With-an-Ax."

Several sentries were stationed among the ancient stone stairs and terraces. They carried a variety of assault rifles, most of them M-16s, and some Soviet-made AK-47s and SKS carbines. The guards had clearly been warned to expect trouble. They paced the walls and watched the surrounding foliage with obvious suspicion.

This won't be easy, Katz thought as he examined the Temple of Parashurama from between the stalks of some ferns.

The Phoenix Force commander lay on his belly, MP-5 subgun pressed against his left side and the steel hooks of his prosthesis beside his right ear. He studied the area, and suddenly looked hard at an odd-looking fern a few yards ahead of him. Its leaves fanned out in an odd heart shape from a thick green stem. It seemed out of place with the other plants. The Israeli knew that there was something else about the fern that bothered him.

He suddenly realized what it was. In the dim light, the fern looked real, but the plastic leaves shone slightly in the moonlight, and the stem was a painted aluminum shaft. It had to be a detection device, probably a motion detector or a radio microphone designed to amplify sound to a receiver unit inside the temple.

Katz stiffened and involuntarily held his breath. If there was one detector at the perimeter of the base, there would certainly be others. The temple of Parashurama was probably surrounded with them. At least one member of the assault force would surely trigger the detectors by a movement or a sound. If the surveillance system was sophisticated enough, it might even register heartbeats or body temperature, even distinguishing human intruders from other large mammals.

Orange flame-bursts of automatic fire from a terrace confirmed Katz's fears. Screams in the bush answered the volleys of bullets.

The enemy knew that Phoenix Force and the PMB had arrived, and they were chopping them down with automatic fire before Phoenix Force and their Indonesian allies could even get into position.

13

Munap Djarios charged up a flight of stone steps inside the temple and along a corridor. Other men darted past him to their defensive positions throughout the building. A couple might have been surprised to see Munap headed in the opposite direction of the battle, but they assumed he had to consult with the colonel about the defenses against the invaders. The *Mérah Tentera* flunkies were too busy to give the matter much thought just then.

Colonel Qui's door was unlocked. Munap opened it and darted inside. The Vietnamese officer stood near his cot, still dressed in an orange robe, arms covered by the flowing sleeves and folded on his chest. Qui looked at Munap and nodded, a grim expression on his round face.

Three other men were in the room. Fong, a short Malay-Chinese more accustomed to forging documents and identification papers than to facing gun battles, sat behind Qui's desk and tried to keep his hands steady enough to paste a photograph into a phony passport. Two other Indonesian terrorists sat on the floor, their heads bowed as if they were asleep. Both had been heavily sedated.

"You know what's happened, Colonel?" Munap asked.

"Of course," Qui answered. "I'd have to be deaf and stupid not to realize we're under attack. Comrade Fong? Are you finished?"

"Ja," Fong announced as he started to rise from the desk. "Yes. I don't know what good this passport will do if we cannot leave the base."

"You really don't have to understand," Qui assured him, gesturing toward the door. "Go get your belongings, Fong."

The Malay-Chinese headed for the door, then sensed something was wrong and eyed Munap suspiciously. He was well aware that the big Indonesian *pentjak-silat* expert was extremely dangerous. Fong did not see Qui unfold his arms and withdraw a length of wire from a sleeve.

The colonel stepped forward and swiftly swung the garrote around the forger's head, tightening the wire loop around the man's neck by yanking the wooden handles hard. The wire bit cleanly into Fong's flesh, and blood squirted from the sliced carotid artery. Fong's eyes bulged, and his mouth opened in a futile effort to gasp. Qui pulled him to the floor and cooly continued to throttle him.

Munap frowned as he watched. He understood why it had to be done, but the sight was repugnant to him. The big Indonesian considered himself a warrior, a soldier in a noble cause. Colonel Qui also spoke of this same cause and the righteous nature of the revolution. The Vietnamese mourned his many comrades who had died during and after the war in his homeland, yet he was willing to kill his Indonesian comrades if their deaths were necessary for the success of their operation.

"Take care of the other two, Munap," Qui instructed as he wiped blood from the wire garrote on Fong's shirt.

"You want them dead?" Munap asked in a hard voice. "Kill them yourself."

"We don't have time to argue." Qui left Fong's corpse and hurried to the desk. The Vietnamese examined the forged passport. "Just do it, Munap."

Munap reluctantly approached the two unconscious men. He reached for the kris on his belt. Kneeling beside the nearest man, he hesitated only a moment before he stabbed him in the heart. The man moaned but barely stirred. Grimly the big Indonesian repeated the grisly business with the second man.

"I know this is hard," Qui told him. "We have to do many hard things in time of war."

"So you've said." Munap had noticed Qui did not seem to find it "hard" to murder Fong.

"Get my trunk," Qui ordered. "I still have one more thing to take care of, and it must be done quickly."

THE GUNMEN of the *Mérah Tentera* blasted the foliage with automatic-weapons fire, apparently concentrating on particular areas, probably chosen according to the information supplied by the movement detectors. Phoenix Force and their allies immediately returned fire. Several terrorists jerked wildly and staggered backward as bullets tore into them. They collapsed in bloodied heaps while other Red Army gunmen ducked behind available cover.

"So much for stealth," Calvin James muttered as he aimed his M-16 and triggered the M-203 attachment.

The grenade shell rocketed into a set of stone figures three terrorists were using for cover. The statues were blown to bits when the 40 mm projectile erupted on impact. So were the trio of terrorists seeking shelter behind them.

The enemy gunmen rose from behind a stone handrail on a flight of stairs. They exposed only enough of their heads and faces to aim their weapons at James's position. They still provided ample targets for Gary Manning as he trained his Bushnell scope on them. When he'd found the closest man's forehead in the cross hairs of his sight,

Manning triggered a 3-round burst. The big 7.62 mm slugs grotesquely lobotomized his head, splattering brains and bone fragments over the other gunman.

The second man tried to duck, but Manning opened fire on him before his head could disappear from view. Two G-3 rounds burst open the top of his skull like a lid along the hairline. His corpse tumbled from the head of the staircase down the steps to collide with another pair of *Mérah Tentera* henchmen who were using a stone post for cover.

The gunmen were bowled over and knocked into the open. Rafael Encizo instantly hosed the terrorist with a volley of 9 mm rounds from his Heckler & Koch submachine gun. Their bodies thrashed about at the foot of the stairs while David McCarter yanked the pin from a concussion grenade and lobbed it at another clutch of terrorists trapped behind a large stone well. Amir Said and two Police Mobile Brigade troops kept the enemy busy with hazing fire long enough for McCarter to throw his grenade.

The explosion threw the terrorists from their cover. One man plunged over the rim of the well. Unfortunately for him, the well had dried up long ago, and only a cluster of weeds cushioned his headfirst fall to the bottom. Sergeant Jatta and other PMB troops followed McCarter's example and lobbed more grenades at the temple. The blasts wrenched loose rock and toppled several stone figures from the front of the building. A shard of shrapnel struck the statue of Parashurama and broke off the head of his stone battle-ax.

"*Nachoda* Mendang! *Djawaban, Nachoda!*" Major Tukarno shouted into his radio to Captain Mendang for reinforcements.

Yakov Katzenelenbogen knew they couldn't wait for the help to arrive. The enemy had been thrown on the defensive. The allies had to keep pressing the fight against their opponents. Experience had taught Katz most terrorists are quick to attack but less skilled in defense, because they are unaccustomed to dealing with opponents who can fight back.

"Let's move in!" the Phoenix Force commander ordered, charging forward.

Katz rushed from the cover of the rain forest and headed toward two disoriented and startled Red Army goons. He fired his MP-5 subgun as he ran, directing a fast diagonal slash of parabellum bullets across the pair. They fell like tenpins in a bowling alley.

Other terrorists aimed at the running Phoenix commander, but the other Phoenix pros were already covering him. Manning and James fired at the terrorists lining the terraces and the stairs, while McCarter and Encizo used their shorter-range submachine guns to dispatch terrorists in front of the temple facade.

Mérah Tentera gunmen crumpled in their own blood as Phoenix Force stormed the grounds, followed by Amir Said and the Police Mobile Brigade. As Katz reached the foot of the stairs, he fired up at a group of terrorists positioned on the landing above. The H&K fire effectively forced the enemy to duck low while Encizo hurled another concussion grenade their way. It exploded at the top of the stairs, tossing terrorists over the handrail and down the stone steps like discarded bags of garbage.

Katz and Encizo dashed up the stairs, followed by Major Tukarno and several other PMB soldiers. More figures appeared on the terraces above. Automatic fire immediately drove them back, except for a couple struck by the bullets. The Israeli reached the landing and flung himself across the last few risers to aim his H&K at the archway while Encizo and Tukarno yanked pins from grenades. Then they simultaneously hurled them at the archway.

GARY MANNING, David McCarter and Amir Said heard the grenades explosions above them as they rushed to the thick wooden double doors on the lower level. The Briton and Said fired at the portholes in the wall near the doors to keep the enemy gunmen there busy while Manning ducked low and rushed to the thick oak barricade.

The Canadian demolitions expert removed a packet of gray doughy material, CV-38, and inserted it along the crack between the doors, sticking a detonator with blasting cap and timer into it. Then he took another packet of white plastic explosive and placed a smaller charge along the hinges of the righthand door. After inserting a detonator in the C-4, he set the timers for both.

He swiftly gathered up his G-3 and ran the length of the wall, jogged around the corner to cover and literally ran into a Red Army terrorist hiding there. The *Mérah Tentera* fanatic was as startled as Manning. He started to raise his Beretta M-12, but the Phoenix commando immediately slammed his rifle against the subgun and pinned it down. Then Manning swung a quick butt-stroke at his opponent's head. The Indonesian managed to raise a shoulder to protect his skull, but the force of the rifle stock knocked the Beretta from his grasp.

The terrorist responded with a heel-of-the-palm stroke to the side of Manning's jaw. The man tried to follow with another *pentjak-silat* stroke with his other hand, but his arm was numb from Manning's earlier blow to it. Manning hardly felt the punch the man threw into his abdomen with the second row of his knuckles in a semiclosed fist.

The Canadian slashed the barrel of his G-3 across his opponent's collarbone. The terrorist groaned and started to fall back, and Manning whipped a butt-stroke in a hard uppercut to the man's solar plexus. He gasped and doubled up, breath bursting from his open mouth. Manning grabbed the terrorist by the hair and yanked his head upward, raising the frame of the rifle under the guy's jaw.

Manning seized the rifle with both hands again and shoved hard. This sent the man stumbling back into a wall, skull first. The Phoenix warrior removed the frame of the G-3 from under the man's chin and allowed the unconscious figure to slump to the ground. At the same moment, he heard the loud bang of the first explosion.

The CV-38 low-velocity blast sounded like an amplified shotgun. The explosion simply cut inward to burst the bolt that held the doors shut. Now they swung open easily from the force of the blast, and the terrorists inside rushed to the threshold to defend themselves. They were unaware of the second charge until the high-velocity C-4 exploded.

About one hundred grams of the compound was more than enough to reduce the door to kindling and to tear apart the three Red Army gunmen. The other door was torn from its hinges and hurled from the opening. For good measure McCarter tossed in a concussion grenade, as well. When it had exploded, the British and Canadian commandos rushed the entrance, closely followed by Amir Said.

CALVIN JAMES SOLVED the problem of getting through a second thick pair of oak doors by blowing them to bits with a 40 mm grenade shell from his M-203. He and two PMB troops headed to the opening. Dead terrorists littered the corridor inside. James entered, his M-16 leading the way.

"How do we handle this, Mr. Jones?" a familiar voice inquired.

James turned and saw Sergeant Jatta was one of the men who had followed him into the temple. He did not recognize the other soldier. James felt uncomfortable about being separated from the other Phoenix commandos, but he found some solace in the knowledge that the PMB were professionals.

"I'll take point," James said. "You back me up and tell the other dude to watch the rear."

Jatta nodded. The black commando held the M-16 at hip level as he advanced. James was also armed with a Beretta 9 mm pistol in shoulder leather and a Muela paramilitary knife in a belt sheath. A high-quality weapon similar to the Ka-Bar survival knife, the Muela has a fifteen-centimeter martensitic steel blade, razor sharp with scalloped saw teeth along the spine. The handle was made of Zamak alloy with nylon grips. James would have been happier with his familar Blackmoor Dirk, but the Spanish fighting knife would be an adequate replacement.

The corridor was narrow and dark, lined with stone walls and sprinkled with spent cartridge casings. James strained his eyes in the dim light and moved toward the electric glow of lights at the end of the hall. The silhouette of a man's figure appeared. James instinctively fired a 3-round burst. The 5.56 mm slugs knocked down the shape as impersonally as shooting a target at a firing range.

James rushed forward, certain that there were more opponents who would try to organize a better defense when they realized what had happened. One grenade in the corridor could wipe out James, Jatta and the other PMB trooper. He reached the mouth of the corridor and dropped to one knee, rifle sweeping from side to side as he scanned the room beyond.

It was too large to properly be called a room. The great hall had once been a place for dozens of worshippers to gather in homage to Parashurama. Another statue of the ax-wielding Hindu god stood on a stone platform, flanked by large brass incense burners and finely carved lions with wide-open jaws and short, curly manes.

Thick pillars stood in strategic rows, and electrical bulbs, powered by a diesel generator, hung from the high ceiling. Stacks of crates and barrels lined one side of the hall, and several dozen cots and duffel bags were arranged in the center. James noted the empty rifle racks where the terrorists' weapons had been stored until the enemy armed themselves to respond to the attack. At the head of the stone steps leading to another hallway above, a lone figure pointed an AK-47 at the corridor. Other men lurked behind pillars and swung weapons at James as he assessed his position. The black commando muttered an oath. He quickly aimed his M-16 and triggered a 3-round burst at the gunman on the stairs.

The terrorist's body jerked as the 5.56 mm slugs struck home. The bullets from his Kalashnikov raked the walls surrounding the mouth of the corridor as he fell. James heard them as they ricocheted against the stone as he dived for the piles of crates for cover. More gunfire chased the commando, sparking against the wall behind him.

Jatta and the other PMB soldier returned fire. James glanced around the crates and saw one terrorist gunman slump beside a pillar. He also noticed that the guy on the stairs now lay dead at the foot of the steps. Jatta darted over to James, firing his H&K MP-5 chattergun as he ran. His bullets struck pillars to keep the enemy at bay, failing to hit any human targets.

The enemy answered with submachine guns. Jatta managed to reach cover by James just as a barrage of gunfire hit the floor at the NCO's heels. One terrorist exposed himself just long enough for the other PMB trooper to nail him with a burst from his Beretta M-12. The soldier saw his opponent fall to the stone floor and ducked for shelter behind the nearest pillar.

An eruption of automatic fire from another terrorist weapon caught the trooper in the side and spun him around to receive a second volley full in the chest. He hit the floor and slid to a wall like a bloodied rag doll. James spotted the head and shoulders of the assassin and snap-aimed his M-16 and fired. The man's head snapped back from the force of the 5.56 mm projectiles, and the Danish-made Madsen chopper was flung from his grasp as he collapsed.

"Watch this end," James told Sergeant Jatta as he moved to the opposite end of the supplies.

He leaned around the new position to examine the area for more terrorists from a different angle. James could not see anyone hiding among the pillars or at the stairs. He extended the barrel of his M-16 and scanned the area with greater care to be certain.

Strong hands suddenly seized the rifle barrel and pulled forcibly. Caught off guard, James hurtled forward, the M-16 ripped from his grasp as he fell into a stack of wooden boxes full of various vegetables and fruits. Those that split open under his weight spilled oranges and pears across the floor in the direction of the American commando.

He glanced up to see the grinning face of Bagus. The diminutive terrorist had allowed his own M-16 to clatter to the floor and raised his more familiar *sumpit* to his lips. James felt his stomach knot as Bagus aimed the blowgun at his face and neck. The weapon was already loaded with a poison dart, and he could not hope to draw his Beretta pistol before Bagus could launch his lethal projectile.

James grabbed a wooden box of oranges in both hands and hauled it in front of his face and head. He gambled that Bagus would try to fire the dart at his neck or perhaps an eyesocket to be certain it delivered its poison to the brain. The dart struck the wooden box with a loud tap. The little crate probably would not have much protection from a bullet, but it stopped the *sumpit* dart.

Bagus snarled as he lunged for the fallen M-16. James hurled the box of oranges at him and caught him in the side of the head, knocking the little terrorist spread-eagled across the floor. He had missed the M-16, but he still held the bamboo blowgun in one fist. He sat up and glared at the American as he hastily jammed another dart into the mouthpiece of his *sumpit*.

James grabbed his Muela knife from his belt sheath and snapped his arm forward to catapult the knife at the terrorist. The steel tip struck him in the chest and neatly split his sternum. Bagus screamed once and fell on his back, blowgun still clenched in his fist.

The Phoenix warrior rushed toward him as Bagus tried to get up. The knife was still lodged in Bagus's chest, but the desperate man tried to raise his weapon to his mouth. James swung a roundhouse kick to the bamboo tube, booting the blowgun out of Bagus's fingers.

"Didn't get to pin me," James panted as he threw another kick. "My turn!"

His boot heel hammered into the butts of the Muela knife handle. The kick drove the blade ten centimeteres deeper into the terrorist's chest. Bagus's mouth fell open, and blood gushed over his shirtfront. James jumped back and watched the terrorist wriggle on the floor briefly before he was still.

"Mr. Jones? Are you all right?" Sergeant Jatta appeared cautiously from the stacks of crates.

"Yeah," James said as he scooped up the M-16. "Come on, man. We got work to do."

The pair moved to the stairs and mounted to the next story. They examined the corridor with care, weapons held ready. It seemed deserted. Three doors stood closed and silent on either side. Sergeant Jatta took a grenade from his belt and prepared to pull the pin as they stood at the end of the hallway.

At that instant an explosion from one of the rooms filled the hallway with a deafening blast and a pounding shock wave. James felt himself lifted into the air and smashed into a wall. Then he sank into oblivion as another explosion rocked the world from somewhere far away.

14

David McCarter paced the tile floor, an unlit cigarette clenched between his teeth. He was still dressed in his fatigue uniform with his Browning in shoulder leather. He had left his H&K submachine gun and grenades on the Chinook that had flown from the Temple of Parashurama to the Lingkaran Military Hospital near Surabaja in East Java.

The emergency staff were ready when the big chopper arrived. McCarter and Gary Manning had carried the stretcher with Calvin James on it themselves. While they paced anxiously, waiting for news of their own wounded from the army doctors, more were delivered to the emergency rooms. Many were Police Mobile Brigade soldiers, but the vast majority were *Mérah Tentera* terrorists.

"What's taking so bloody long?" McCarter complained as he marched in a circle once more.

"It seems like a long time," Manning replied. He sat on a chair and stared into the cup of black coffee in his hands. "But it's only been twenty minutes. The staff are busy as hell right now. They'll have to give first priority to treating all the wounded. They can't take time out to tell us what kind of condition Cal is in."

"Well, they'd better see to him before they do as much as put a bloody Band-Aid on any of those damned terrorists,'' the Briton hissed. ''Stinking scum are lucky we even brought them in for medical treatment....''

He realized his temper was making him say things he did not really believe. McCarter pulled the cigarette from his mouth and threw it into a trash can. Manning understood what McCarter was feeling because the same emotions were gnawing at his gut.

Rafael Encizo and Yakov Katzenelenbogen approached their teammates. The Cuban and Israeli warriors had arrived in the second Chinook with yet more injured men. Encizo asked if they had heard anything about James, and he looked relieved that they had not been told anything yet. He figured that no news was better than learning their friend and fellow warrior was dead.

''I know this is hard,'' Katz announced quietly, ''but some of us have to head back to the temple to inspect the area for files, records, possible identification of the Djarios brothers and that sort of thing.''

''Jesus!'' McCarter snapped. ''Can't that bleedin' wait? Those bastards are dead. They're not going anywhere, and their damned files will still be there after we find out if our mate is going to make it or not!''

''I'm as upset about this as the rest of you,'' Katz assured him, ''but we still have a job to do, and it isn't over yet.''

''Yeah,'' McCarter replied, and shook his head. ''I know. I know you're right.''

''I'd rather have some work to do than sit here and worry,'' Manning stated. He rose from his chair. ''I'll fly back with...''

Major Turkano marched in and gestured for the four Phoenix commandos to move in so their conversation would not be overheard.

"I spoke with two doctors who are taking care of Mr. Jones," Tukarno stated. "They said he's suffered from several shrapnel wounds in the torso and arms, but none seems life threatening."

"Seems?" Encizo asked. "What's that mean?"

"Too early to tell," the major answered. "Jones is still unconscious, but they don't see any evidence of injury to his skull or neck. They're still worried about internal bleeding and possible infections, but they're fairly sure he'll be all right. Your friend won't be going anywhere for a while. Be assured he'll get the best possible care."

"Thank you, Major," Katz said with a sigh of relief. "We appreciate that. We're also very sorry about Sergeant Jatta."

"He was a very good man," Tukarno said sadly. "He served with me for the last five years. The sergeant was my friend, as well as my aide. May Allah grant him every wish and reward in paradise."

"I sincerely hope so," Katz said, "but I'm afraid we still have some work to do before the night is over."

"I'll come along, too," Encizo volunteered. "I've done some forensic work over the years and may be able to help the lab people."

"So you want me to stay here and check on Jones's condition?" McCarter inquired.

"Why not?" Encizo said with a shrug. "We passed a soft-drink machine with Coca-Cola among the selections. You should be okay."

"That's cute," McCarter said sourly. "Do any of the doctors speak English?"

"There are some other guys here who do," Amir Said remarked as he shuffled near the group. "I saw them talking to somebody at the administration office. Three white men in single-breasted suits. One of them is named Chappell, or at least that's the name he used to go by when I knew him."

"Shit," McCarter muttered. "CIA?"

"That's who I used to work for," Said confirmed. "Obviously they must have heard about tonight's raid. Automatic fire and explosions on an island the size of Bali are bound to be noticed. The Chinooks flying here didn't make it too hard for CIA and probably NSA—maybe even KGB and whatever other intelligence networks are operating in Indonesia—to track us."

"So what do we do now?" Manning asked with a sigh.

"This isn't totally unexpected," Katz remarked as he scratched the whisker stubble on his chin with the hooks of his prosthesis. "Amir, perhaps you should introduce me to Mr. Chappell."

"They didn't see me," Said explained. "We might be able to slip away...."

"Mr. Jones isn't going anywhere," Katz stated. "Neither are the other injured we hauled in here tonight. That includes a number of terrorists, as well as the PMB soldiers. There's just so much we can cover up at this point. I think it's time we contact the Company, anyway. They're old hands at coverups."

"They're probably better at covering up facts than getting information," Encizo muttered. The Bay of Pigs veteran did not have a very high opinion of the CIA.

"You go to the temple with Miller and see what you can find, Ramirez," Katz told him. He did not like to have the Cuban in the same room with CIA personnel unless it was necessary. "I'll meet with Chappell. Major Tukarno, you can stay or leave. If you stay, I'm afraid you'll have to talk to CIA, as well."

"I'd like to be here at the hospital to hear about the condition of my men," Tukarno replied. "A couple of them may not make it through the night, and I don't want them to die alone. Perhaps I can ease their final journey by reading a passage from the Koran and join them in prayer. If a man is sedated or unconscious, I'll pray for him alone. If I must also meet with the CIA in order to do this, I suppose that is a small sacrifice compared to what my fellow soldiers have given this night.''

"You might want to take something for nausea when you talk to them," Encizo said dryly. "If the Company sends anyone to the Temple of Parashurama, tell them not to get in our way."

"By the time they get around to sending anybody, you guys will be finished with the place and examining evidence under microscopes in Djakarta," Said assured him. "I'd rather go with you than meet with Chappell again."

"Sorry, Amir," Katz told the ex-CIA agent. "You're our contact with this fellow."

"Hell," McCarter muttered. "I don't mind talking to those bastards. We've got White House authority, so they can kiss my arse. Let them get high and mighty, and I'll tell those..."

"You stay here," Katz insisted. "Get a Coke and find a place to smoke a cigarette and calm down. Jones will be all right, and we'll take care of the CIA."

"Just tell the silly sods we did their ruddy job and then some."

"I don't know why you didn't go into the diplomatic corps," Manning told him, and shook his head with dismay.

ROBERT CHAPPELL WAS a tall, thin man with a lean face and features that seemed pinched together in a permanently sour expression. The CIA control officer looked as if he had sucked the most bitter lemon in history and had never recovered from the taste. His expression seemed to grow steadily more acetous as he listened to Katz in a small private room by the hospital administration offices.

"This is the biggest pile of crap I've heard for a long time, Colby," Chappell remarked, and shifted a hard stare in Said's direction. "What kind of outfit did you wind up with, Amir? If you think I believe this garbage about getting authority directly from the Oval Office..."

"Please check our claim," Katz invited. "I believe you can do that by contacting your control officer in Thailand. He'll have to go through Code Blue Alpha Twelve clearance with that high-tech decoding machine. You might let him know because that will save him some time."

"Who the hell are you people?" another CIA man named Finaly inquired. His rugged face, highlighted by a broken nose, resembled the Hollywood version of a thug rather than a secret agent. "What do you think you're doing carrying out a covert operation with Indonesian military personnel without going through the Company or National Security Agency ops that have been here since 1960?"

"I've already explained that two NSA agents were killed in Borneo, so we couldn't be sure that any American intel personnel here were safe contacts," Katz said with a sigh. "However, the evidence we've uncovered suggests the *Mérah Tentera* killed them simply because they were Americans, and the terrorists had no knowledge that either victim was involved in covert operatons or planning to establish a listening post in Borneo."

"Well, thank you for sharing that little piece of information with us," Chappell said sarcastically. "You could have done that before you went to Bali and shot up the place. What is this cowboy crap? Don't you realize Bali is the major tourist attraction in Indonesia? You've endangered dozens of innocent American lives with that attack.''

''Would you object if only Indonesian lives had been in jeopardy?'' Major Tukarno asked dryly.

''Of course I would,'' Chappell answered. ''We are concerned for your country and your people, Major. One might wonder how much concern you have for agreeing to work with these five mystery men.''

''These men have done a fine job here, and they've probably saved a lot of lives—Indonesian as well as American,'' Tukarno replied. ''The riot at the Embassy probably would have been far bloodier if they had not been present.''

''That incident sure had us running around like decapitated chickens,'' a Company man named Hansen admitted. ''We figured out the terrorists started the riot by shooting at the demonstrators, but then we couldn't find out who took care of the terrorists.''

Chappell stared hard at Hansen. The senior man didn't like one of his people even hinting that there was anything admirable about anyone who handled covert operations without going through the Company.

''May I remind you, Mr. Chappell,'' Tukarno began, ''that Indonesia is my country, not yours. I am convinced we acted in the best interest of my country and protected American interests here, as well. Whether or not you agree, I don't really care.''

''A gun battle at a tourist center like Bali was in our mutual best interests?'' Chappell asked, raising one eyebrow.

''Oh, ease up on that shit, Bob,'' Amir Said told him. ''The attack was launched against a terrorist base at an abandoned temple, and the only people who got hurt were terrorists and some damned fine soldiers who knew the risks and were willing to take them. No tourists or Indonesian civilians were ever at risk."

"You never did like going by the rules, Amir," Chappell accused the former agent. "This sort of mission probably tickled the hell out of you. Get a chance to show up the Company? Give us a little tweak on the nose?"

"This isn't about the Company, Bob," Said replied. "You always take everything personally. We didn't involve the CIA for the same reason you guys don't involve the American public. There was no 'need to know,' so we didn't tell you."

"But you're telling us now that it's over?" Chappell inquired. "It is over? Right?"

"We're not sure yet," Katz admitted. "There were about sixty terrorists there. They were well armed, they had sophisticated surveillance gear, and they put up quite a fight. One of my men was injured, and Major Tukarno's aide was killed in an explosion in a room reported to be the office of a mysterious character known as 'the colonel.' We don't know if it was caused by a booby trap or triggered by an exploding grenade. Sergeant Jatta was apparently hit by the blast as he pulled the pin from a grenade. The explosion threw him down a flight of stairs, and the grenade went off in his hand."

"So it's possible your man had already thrown a grenade at the door?" Chappell asked with a frown.

"The office was at the end of the corridor, and using a grenade to blast a door is fairly standard," Katz answered. "It knocks out any booby traps or brings down anyone who might be waiting behind it. But in this case the explosion was more powerful than usual in booby traps. Since Jones is unconscious, he can't tell us if he lobbed a grenade or not. We suspect he didn't, and the bomb went off on its own."

"Did you check the office afterwards?" Chappell asked.

"Briefly. We had injured to take care of and prisoners to round up. That's why we sent a team back to investigate. We did find the remains of three bodies. The corpses, or what was left of them, in the office seem to fit the general descriptions of Hasan and Munap Djarios and the colonel. The bodies seemed to be about the right height, build and age. Part of one man's face was intact, and his features seemed to be Malay-Chinese, and the arm of the largest victim had a tattoo of a kris. Munap Djarios has a tattoo like that, according to his file, and the colonel is believed to be a Malay-Chinese."

"Well, then, congratulations," Chappell announced with an exaggerated expression. "You killed off the big bad leaders of the terrorist movement. Now you can go home."

"Sorry to disappoint you," Katz replied. "We're not leaving with one of our people in the hospital. Besides, we still have to find out the answers to a few nagging questions. Something about this business still bothers me."

"Such as?" Chappell demanded, his eyes wide, as if trying to force Katz to speak by the sheer power of his will.

"Well, it seemed the terrorists expected trouble," the Phoenix commander answered. "It was as if they knew we were coming or strongly suspected it. The sentries were fully prepared and alert. Detectors ringed the area, and they all had weapons in hand when we hit."

"You did take a terrorist prisoner at the Embassy," Hansen reminded him. "They probably figured you got the guy to talk. Good guess because that's exactly what you did."

"True," Katz agreed. "But if they expected trouble, why did they stay at the base to fight us? If the colonel or the Djarios brothers were smart enough to figure out that we'd come after them, they should have been smart enough to know we'd arrive in force to take care of whatever opposition we found there. Why didn't they leave the area? There's a harbor nearby. They could have fled to Borneo or across the Bali Sea to Java."

"You tried to hit them as fast as possible," Chappell said with a shrug. "Maybe you got there before they could pack up and haul ass."

"I would like to believe that," Katz assured him. "I'd also like to know why three men would commit suicide with a bomb...if that's what happened at the colonel's office."

"An explosion would be quick and pretty painless," Finaly remarked. "It sounds like they used enough explosives to do the job."

"Yeah," Said confirmed, "but most of the damage from the explosion was at the door. Wouldn't you think a fella would sit on a bomb if he really wanted to blow himself up?"

"Of course, the explosion did mangle and mutilate the corpses quite badly," Katz added. "There was enough left to make a basic identification. The arm with the tattoo happened to be under a desk so it didn't get mutilated, even though the fingers were missing, and naturally, so are the dead man's fingerprints. Some very odd coincidences."

"Oh, God," Chappell snorted, and rolled his eyes toward the ceiling. "You got the sons of bitches, and it's over. So what if there's an odd coincidence or two? You got odd coincidences in everyday life, for Christ's sake."

"You may be right," Katz admitted. "If it was one or two coincidences, I might agree with you. However, we want to make sure we finish our mission before we leave Indonesia."

"Well," Chappell said with a sigh, "I reckon we use some different methods, but we're still on the same side. I'm still going to check you guys out as best as I can. If you really have White House authority, the Company will help you any way it can. If you don't . . . then your ass is grass and I'm the lawnmower."

Amir Said laughed and shook his head.

"What's so funny?" Chappell demanded.

"Colby and the other four men in his team have been in three firefights in two days," Said answered. "They've taken on multiple opponents armed with automatic weapons and grenades, and barely batted an eyelash. Now, you think they're going to be scared of you? What you plan to do, Bob? Deport them back to America?"

"Amir," Katz said quietly, "I appreciate your comments, but you and Major Tukarno and his PMB forces were with us, as well. You all deserve as much credit as we do for whatever success this mission has had so far. Mr. Chappell is welcome to check out our claims. He obviously believes us, anyway, or this conversation wouldn't have been this open, but he can certainly do what he feels necessary for CIA security. Meantime, the best thing the Company can do is use its influence to try to keep details about the incident from leaking to the press for a while. That wouldn't be good for us, and it wouldn't be good for the Company or U.S. relations with Indonesia right now."

"I'll agree with that," Chappell said reluctantly. "I just hope you guys won't be in Southeast Asia much longer."

"We'll be here as long as it takes to be sure our job is finished," Katz informed him. "It's as simple as that."

15

Sergeant Mudo stared at the video screen as information appeared on it. The PMB computer technician grunted and translated the data into English for Yakov Katzenelenbogen and Gary Manning.

"We have some identifications from fingerprints taken from the terrorists at Bali," Mudo explained. "Alive and dead. You can check names and other details on the printout sheets, but the most interesting information is that a number of these Red Army vermin were once inmates at Ek Penjara."

"The same prison the Djarios brothers and some of the other terrorists spent some time in," Manning mused as he sipped a cup of strong black Java coffee. "Not too surprising. Back in the U.S. the Aryan Brotherhood and similar criminal outfits do most of their recruiting in the joint. No reason why terrorists couldn't use the same method."

"Another thing many of these trash have in common is they found employment with small commercial fisherman outfits," Mudo continued.

"Small fishing business like the one operated by the late Mr. Chin?" Katz inquired. "The unfortunate Mr. Chin who hired the Djarios brothers and then went down at sea?"

"Exactly. In fact, these little fishing vessels seemed quite accident-prone with ex-convicts aboard. A boat owned by a guy called Choy went down in the Java Sea. Another one run by one Chu-Lung went up the Makassar Strait and never returned. The ex-convicts aboard were listed as 'missing and presumed dead,' but since no bodies were found, their files were not closed. Now we know what happened to them."

"The men who owned the fishing boats were named Chin, Choy and Chu-Lung," Katz said thoughtfully. "All Chinese."

"Malay-Chinese own many businesses in Indonesia," Major Tukarno commented. He was standing beside the Phoenix Force commander. "That's not terribly uncommon."

"But the man the terrorists called the colonel is also supposed to be a Malay-Chinese," Katz reminded the PMB officer. "I think we've discovered a pattern, Major. I think we've also discovered how *Mérah Tentera* gained its military expertise and new-found cunning. It was because the colonel fell in with the Djarios brothers and gave them a perfect cover. They were officially dead, and so were several other former inmates from Ek Penjara. That's an excellent way to get parole officers and the authorities off your back. No one keeps tabs on dead men."

"Maybe that's what the colonel and the Djarios brothers are counting on once again," Manning remarked. The big Canadian gulped down the last of his coffee and added, "They could have faked their own deaths at the Temple of Parashurama."

Rafael Encizo and Amir Said entered the safehouse and joined the others in time to hear Manning's theory. Tukarno nodded a silent greeting to the new arrivals.

"Mr. Miller has proposed an interesting notion," the major stated. "But this time we don't have bodies lost at sea. We have three corpses that fit the general descriptions of the Red Army leaders. One of them has a tattoo identical to Munap Djarios's. Until we know otherwise, that's fairly convincing evidence he's dead.''

"Not anymore," Encizo announced. "We just came from the autopsies. Your lab personnel in forensics have confirmed the kris tattoo on the dead man's arm was less than twelve hours old. It wasn't the same one Munap got in prison years ago.''

"Indeed?" Tukarno raised an eyebrow. "That is interesting.''

"That's just the beginning," Said assured him. "The autopsies also found that the corpse with the tattoo and the one believed to be Hasan Djarios had both received large doses of Thorazine. On top of that, they had both been stabbed through the heart, and they don't think the wounds were caused by shrapnel. The medical examiner said the puncture wounds appeared to be precise and 'neatly' carried out. His term, not mine. He thinks the weapon was probably a double-edged kris.''

"The body of the man believed to be the colonel is also interesting," Encizo added. "He probably was Malay-Chinese, but he wasn't killed in the explosion. Someone garroted him from behind.''

"May Allah grant us a lamp to dispel the darkness," Tukarno remarked. "It seems we now have proof the leaders are still alive. But how did they escape from the temple?''

"Some of your men found a tunnel that extends under the building," Encizo explained. "It opens near a small harbor along the coast. If they didn't tell the others about it, the tunnel would have been a perfect escape route.''

"They're starting to interrogate some of the healthier terrorists at headquarters," Said declared. "The *Mérah Tentera* goons haven't been very cooperative, but a couple of them did gloat about the fact we didn't get a lot of their comrades because they left a few hours before we arrived at the temple."

"They didn't say where the men went?" Manning inquired.

"No," Said replied. "Apparently no one told them. Hasan just quietly rounded up a bunch of his flunkies and took them somewhere."

"And the rest were sacrificed to try to convince us we'd destroyed the Red Army," Katz commented. He took out a pack of Camels and shook a cigarette loose. "No doubt they intend to remain in hiding for a few months and resume their activities after we've left Indonesia and the PMB's attention turns to more conventional domestic troubles."

"They almost got away with it," said Encizo. "The medical examiners admitted they wouldn't have carried out precise autopsies on bodies that seemed so obviously to have been killed by an explosion if we hadn't insisted on it."

"Unfortunately you gentlemen won't be able to stay here indefinitely," Tukarno said with a sigh. "This is pretty much a problem of the Police Mobile Brigade from here on. It will probably take us months to track down the terrorists to their new lair...wherever that might be."

"Too bad," Sergeant Mudo said with a feeble smile. "The president—that is the Indonesian president—had already extended his congratulations to the Police Mobile Brigade for bringing the business to an end. Someone in the government has also released a statement to the press that assures them that the PMB has been successful against the terrorists."

"You might get a promotion to colonel," Said told Tukarno. "I'd say you deserve it, Major."

"I'd feel better about it if the job was really finished," Tukarno answered. He looked at Katz and frowned. "You and your men are really responsible for what success we've had thus far. You really deserve the credit, but no one will know because your team works in such tight secrecy."

"We'll know, and so will a few people who matter," Encizo assured him. "Besides, the results are what's important. Not who gets the credit."

A phone on Tukarno's desk rang. The major answered the right one on the first try, speaking in English because his mind was still focused on the interrupted conversation. Tukarno was surprised when the caller also responded in English.

"The others are here, Mr. Collins," Tukarno spoke into the phone. "I'll tell them. Thank you."

He hung up and turned to face the three Phoenix Force members. "Collins" was McCarter's cover name, and he was still at the hospital waiting to hear about Calvin James's condition. The other Phoenix pros could not read Tukarno's expression.

"The doctors have confirmed that Mr. Jones has not suffered any head, neck or spinal injury," Tukarno declared. "He had two broken ribs, some sprains and bruises and shallow cuts and punctures from the shrapnel, but no internal bleeding. A shot of penicillin was all that was needed to deal with any infections. He's now regained consciousness, and the doctors assured Collins your friend will be fine. They just want him to stay for at least forty-eight hours before they release him from the hospital."

"Thank God," Katz said with relief.

"I wish he was here," Said commented. "Maybe he could give some of the captive terrorists scopolamine to find out where the rest of them might be hiding. Do you have anyone else who can use scopolamine with the same expertise as Jones, Major?''

"Not that I know of," Tukarno admitted. "I don't know it would do any good, anyway. Truth serum can't make men tell us something they don't know."

"Before we get too depressed," Manning began as he moved to a wall map of Indonesia, "let's consider what might be the most logical places for them to head. Now, the harbor at the Temple of Parashurama was on the coast of the Bali Sea. The nearest spot for them to go would be east to Lombok Island, west to Java or north to Kangean Island."

"Unless they decided to just go to another part of Bali," Tukarno remarked, and shook his head. "They could have headed anywhere within four hundred kilometers. By now, they could have gone anywhere in Indonesia."

"What about Krakatau?" Encizo inquired. "Isn't that an island east of Java?"

"No, it's not," Said declared with a smile. "But I know where you got that idea. There was a movie made in the 1960s that revolved around the great volcanic eruption and earthquakes that occurred at Krakatau in 1883. It was an enormous natural disaster that literally whittled the island down from forty-seven square kilometers to its present sixteen kilometers. What's amusing about the movie version is the title of the film actually claimed Krakatau to be east of Java. Take a look at the map and you'll see Krakatau—at least what's left of it—to the west of Java."

"Somebody actually made a movie with that kind of mistake in the title?" Mudo asked, stunned by this information. "Didn't anyone check where Krakatau is located before they released the movie? What kind of movie was it?"

"One that doesn't have anything to do with our present problem," Major Tukarno told his NCO. "We still have no idea where the terrorists might be."

"Do you remember our conversation with Barinjin?" Katz inquired. "Didn't he say that the two so-called wild-life photographers were killed in Borneo just because the terrorists needed a couple of dead Americans for their terror campaign and because the photographers just *happened* to be in Borneo?"

"Which suggests that Borneo was a convenient base for the Red Army," Manning declared, instantly picking up Katz's train of thought.

"That's a very big assumption, gentlemen," Tukarno said grimly. "Besides, they'd have to travel across the width of the Java Sea. More than four hundred fifty kilometers."

"The large group that left with Hasan Djarios had quite a head start, and no one was looking for them," Katz stated. "Munap and the colonel may still be on their way to Borneo even as we speak. Or they could have gotten to a bush plane on one of the islands between Bali and Borneo."

"Maybe it's worth a try," Tukarno allowed. "But Borneo is enormous. It's nearly 750,000 square kilometers, and only the Kalimantan portion is part of Indonesia. Sabah and Sarawak are Malaysian states, with the nation of Brunei lodged between them. The PMB has no jurisdiction in those territories."

"Kalimantan is larger than all the other parts of Borneo put together," Said reminded him. "Hell, Brunei may be an independent nation, but it's a sultanate no larger than the state of Delaware."

"The terrorists may have their base there, nonetheless," Tukarno insisted. "My point is we're dealing with an enormous area and possibly with territories that are not part of Indonesia.''

''Excuse me,'' Mudo interrupted. ''The fishing boats owned by Choy and Chu-Lung were both in port at Kalimantan harbors before they were lost at sea. If these were aliases used by the colonel, it suggests he was familiar with Borneo and may have established connections there.''

''He's not the only one with connections,'' Said announced. ''I have some friends and relatives in Borneo. They wouldn't be willing to talk to the Police Mobile Brigade, but they'll talk to me.''

''Criminals?'' Tukarno demanded, his tone dripping with accusation.

''Let's just say they have personal reasons for wishing to avoid contact with the police,'' Said replied.

''If they can help us find the terrorists, that's good enough for us,'' Katz declared. ''Amir mentioned them before. They're not drug dealers, murder incorporated or anything that's a genuine threat to Indonesia. The same cannot be said about the Red Army terrorists.''

''All right,'' Tukarno agreed, reluctantly. ''If they can help, you may use them, Amir.''

''Frankly I'd do it with or without your permission,'' Said responded with a shrug. ''I just hope the Company doesn't poke their nose into this. Chappell knows about some of my contacts from when I was in the CIA. I'm not sure if he knows about those in Borneo or not.''

''Let's hope the CIA will slosh about in its own bureaucracy for a while,'' Katz remarked. ''They seem pretty eager to close the whole business and get rid of us. Of course, that may be because they intend to start their own investigations of the *Mérah Tentera*.''

''First the CIA will want to find out about us in the hope that we won't actually have White House authority. They'll want to get even with us for stealing their thunder," Encizo said dryly. "They'll try to have some excuses lined up to explain why they've been ineffective while we've made progress. They'll also assume we're NSA, and they'll start trying to get information from the National Security Agency stations here in Indonesia."

"That sounds about right," Said agreed. "Were you in the Company once, Ramirez?"

"Bite your tongue! I think we ought to pick up Collins at the hospital and head to Borneo as soon as possible."

"Right," Katz confirmed. "Let's do it."

16

The morning sun stood above the treetops of an ebony forest beyond the river settlement. Clouds hung in the sky like islands of cotton against the clear blue. The village's simple wooden dwellings were mounted on poles and pallets in case the Barito River flooded during the rainy months of October through May. The reflections of the elevated houses shimmered in the water as sunlight glittered across the surface.

The temperature was roughly eighty degrees, but the humidity was muggy and oppressive. The men of Phoenix Force were no strangers to tropical climates. Many of their missions had taken them to Africa, Central and South America, Asia and the Middle East. Yet even Rafael Encizo—who despised cold weather and preferred hot climates—found the sweltering conditions physically trying. Amir Said mopped his brow with a sleeve and glanced at the four supercommandos. They were holding up well in the Borneo heat.

"The precipitation level here is incredible," Said informed his companions. "More than twenty-five hundred milimeters is the average for the whole island, and some areas get more than that."

"Maybe we'll be on *Jeopardy* some day and the category will be 'Miserable Weather Throughout the World,'"

David McCarter muttered. The Briton shifted the strap of his duffel bag to prevent it cutting into his shoulder.

"How much farther, Amir?" Katz inquired. The Israeli held the shoulder strap to a duffel bag with his single fist as he used the hooks of his prosthesis to pull down the brim of a straw hat.

"We're almost there," Said assured him.

"Didn't you say that ten minutes ago?" Gary Manning asked. The powerful Canadian had great reserves of stamina, but even his endurance was wearing thin.

"Was that only ten minutes ago?" Encizo commented wearily.

The four Phoenix commandos and Said had trekked through kilometers of rain forest after they had arrived at an airstrip shortly after sunrise. Said led them to the settlement approximately sixty kilometers north of Bandjarmasin, which is the closest thing to a major city one will find in Borneo.

As they headed along the plank walkways toward the houses on stilts, a great white building with a handsome dome and four minarets rose in the distance. The mosque seemed out of place in the midst of the shabby housing. Apparently the villagers were willing to live in slum conditions and worship Allah in a beautiful huge building of white stone and marble. Perhaps the poor have a greater need for religion, with its spiritual strength and hope for a better eternity to compensate for the miseries of the present.

A group of Dayak villagers were creating batik fabric in front of the dwellings. The Dayaks are the original aboriginal inhabitants of Borneo, but batik is made throughout Indonesia. The women carefully applied patterns of melted wax to the fabric, and the men dipped it in vegetable dye. When the wax is removed, designs appear on the fabrics.

Phoenix Force followed Said past the villagers to a large, drab building. Like most of the Dayak dwellings, it had a wide, slanted roof above a porch so the frequent and heavy rainfall could run off. However, the dwelling Said selected had tinted-glass windows instead of screens, and the door was made of thick metal painted to resemble wood.

"Rasul?" Said spoke as he knocked on the door. "It's Amir with some friends."

"Siapa?" a voice called from behind the door.

"Amir Said, that's who," the former CIA agent repeated. "Look out the peephole, Rasul."

The door opened, and a short dark figure dressed in a white silk house robe smiled at Said. His wide aboriginal features seemed pleasant, although he carried a Madsen submachine gun under one arm.

"My old chap, Amir!" Rasul greeted. He spoke English with an exaggerated British accent that sounded like a bad American actor attempting to imitate the late James Mason. "Quite good to see you again, old boy. I see we have guests. English? American? Australian, perhaps?"

"They all speak English, Rasul," Said replied. "That's all you really need to know for right now."

"That's fine," Rasul announced with a broad grin. "For right now. Do come in. Bit of a scorcher out there today, eh?"

Phoenix Force and Said entered the house, their eyes adjusting to the darker interior. The room contrasted dramatically with the outside of the dwelling. The spacious front room was furnished with a long white sofa, two armchairs, a glass-top coffee table and an entertainment center boasting a large color television set, VCR and stereo with massive speakers. Two beautiful Moluccan cockatoos shared a wide perch at one end of the room. The large hook-bills had food trays, water and toys. One of the large white birds raised its crest feathers slightly and puffed out its body, alarmed by the visitors. The other simply stretched out its neck and cocked its head to one side to calmly observe the arrivals.

Cool air washed over the men, a great relief after the past two hours in the blistering heat. They understood why Rasul had glass windows and kept his door closed; his house was air-conditioned. Rasul gestured at the furniture.

"Please relax," he invited. "May I get you some beverage? Iced coffee? Tea? I may have a bit of beer on stock. Keep it for non-Muslim visitors."

"You have any Coca-Cola?" McCarter asked hopefully.

"As a matter of fact, I do," Rasul replied happily. "You sound like you're from the East End of London. I've been there from time to time. Lovely city, but I prefer Singapore. You can do just about anything and find just about anything you need if you know the right people in Singapore."

"Right now we need information about some people here in Borneo," Katz interrupted politely. "Amir has spoken quite highly of you. He says nothing happens here without your knowledge."

"A frightful exaggeration, I'm afraid," Rasul replied, looking pleased. "However, I am not without certain sources of information that may be available for the right price. Let's say one hundred thousand rupiah? A thousand Singapore dollars would suit me even better."

"A thousand American dollars would be twice as much," McCarter stated. "I'm sure that would suit you well enough when you make your next trip to Singapore."

"My, yes," Rasul confirmed with a grin. "Tell me what you need to know, and I shall do my very best to supply that information, gentlemen."

"We're trying to locate a secret base of the *Mérah Tentera*," Encizo explained.

"I don't do business with terrorists," Rasul said with a frown. "Surely Amir informed you of this."

"No one is suggesting you do," Katz assured him. "We think there may be a terrorist base here in Borneo."

"I haven't heard anything about a base," Rasul declared. "Mind you, those terrorist buggers have been active here. Killed two American blokes out in the mangroves. But if they have a base here in Borneo, I don't know about it."

"We suspect a number of men arrived in Borneo by boat sometime between 11 p.m. and maybe as late as four or five in the morning," Manning remarked. "Between twenty-five to fifty men. Sometimes later, perhaps after dawn, two or more men arrived."

"Boats come in and out of harbor all the time," Rasul stated. "They go up the rivers inland. However, I take it these men you seek would not wish to be observed. They wouldn't use one of the standard ports of commercial industry and transportation?"

"They'd probably favor the same sort of quiet little coves smugglers would be apt to use," Encizo said with a nod.

"Are these blokes Dayaks?" Rasul inquired.

"As far as we know, they're mostly from Java and Sumatra," Amir answered. "Although it is possible some are Balinese, Dayaks or even Irians."

"You didn't say Iranians, did you?" Encizo inquired. The Cuban was finding himself frequently annoyed and confused in Indonesia.

"Irians," Said repeated. "Individuals who live in West Irian or, as you might call it, the west section of the island of New Guinea. The east portion is now part of Papua New Guinea, but the West Irian portion is still under Indonesian authority."

"That's what I thought you meant," Encizo said with a shrug.

"But the fellows you're looking for would be a bit of a mixed lot from the other islands," Rasul said thoughtfully. "Being terrorists, I reckon they'd carry weapons or something they could hide weapons in. I know a few blokes along the coast who may have noticed some chaps like that if they really did arrive here. You fellows don't seem positive about that yourselves."

"You're right," Katz admitted. "It's sort of an educated guess that may prove to be wrong."

"For a thousand dollars I'll see what I can turn up," Rasul assured them. "You do understand, I must receive five hundred up front? Business is business, as they say, and I'll have to pay my informants whether they turn up anything or not."

"Rasul is man of honor," Said told Phoenix Force. "In his own way, of course."

"Men of honor deserve to make a profit," Katz stated. "I just hope your friend will be successful."

"I'll find out," Rasul announced cheerfully. "If you'll excuse me, I'll get to my transceiver radio and see about contacting my mates along the coast. This may take two or three hours. Perhaps longer. Amir knows where the kitchen is. If you're hungry, convince him to prepare *sate kambing* with *nasi goréng*. I have all the ingredients in the fridge, but I've never had much of a knack as a cook."

"That's charcoal-broiled lamb with fried rice," Said explained. "If the rest of you are hungry..."

"Personally I'd rather use the two or three hours to take a nap than eat," Katz replied. "We've all been up all night, and the last twenty-four hours have been rather hectic. I think I'll do my body a favor and get some sleep."

"I'm a bit too keyed up to sleep," McCarter stated.

"Trying to run on adrenaline gets steadily harder the older you get," Katz told him. "You'll find out when you hit fifty. Or should I say *if* you hit fifty?"

"Considering the nature of our profession," the Briton replied with a shrug, "I just reckon I ought to concern myself with surviving one day at a time."

"Yeah," Encizo added. "Some days that's tougher than others."

YAKOV KATZENELENBOGEN enjoyed the luxury of four hours of sleep before Amir Said woke him. The Israeli had taken a nap on the sofa, his prosthesis and 9 mm Beretta M-92 on the coffee table within easy reach. Said had only to speak Katz's current cover name to wake the Phoenix commander.

"You're a light sleeper, Colby," Said remarked as he placed a cup of hot coffee on the table.

"An acquired trait," Katz answered. He sat up and stretched his neck and shoulders. The empty sleeve swung loosely at the stump of his right arm. "Rasul have any luck?"

"So it seems," Said replied. "He had to use the bathroom, but he'll explain everything when he comes back."

Katz was surprised to notice McCarter curled up in one of the armchairs, sound asleep. Manning lay on the floor with his duffel bag for a pillow. Said smiled and handed the coffee to Katz.

"Your friends decided to follow your example," he remarked.

"Good," Katz said as he sipped the coffee. He would have preferred tea, but he appreciated Said's thoughtfulness. "Where's Ramirez?"

"In the kitchen sharpening his knives," Said answered. "I like a man who appreciates a good blade."

The ex-CIA man patted the parang in a cross-draw sheath on his belt. Said always carried the big jungle knife when he ventured into the rain forests. Since it was used as a weapon in *pentjak-silat* martial arts, as well as a tool, the parang was a particularly practical item.

Rasul entered the room, a long dark cigar jutting from his grinning mouth. He strolled over to the unoccupied armchair and seated himself across from Katz. The wheeler-dealer glanced at the prosthesis on the coffee table. Rasul was intrigued by the hard plastic shell of the artificial forearm that shielded steel levers and cables. The straps at the cupped end of the device revealed how the prosthesis was attached to Katz's abbreviated right arm.

"I've always wondered how those things work," Rasul commented.

"It has a few limitations and a few advantages," Katz told him. "When I first lost my arm, I learned about some of the limitations, but the longer I used the prosthesis, the more I realized those limitations were fewer than you might think. Thanks to new technology, prosthetic devices get better every year."

"What sort of advantages does it have?" Rasul inquired.

"Oh, I can open wine bottles without a corkscrew," Katz answered. "Move charcoals on a barbecue without burning my fingers. The hooks can also do some damage to human flesh and bone if the need arises."

"I can imagine," Rasul said as he looked at the steel talons with respect. "I'm sure you must be more interested in what I learned from my mates along the coast than discussing a matter that's probably a bit boring for you.''

"A bit boring for all of us," Encizo remarked as he appeared from the kitchen. The Cuban slid the big Muela Bowie knife into the belt sheath as he approached. "I hope your friends came up with something to spare us further ennui.''

"A fellow called Djagal runs a small private import/ export trade at a small cove a few kilometers east of Cape Selatan," Rasul began. "Last night, actually about one o'clock in the morning, a fishing boat arrived with a group of men. About forty, Djagal claims. He didn't get too close, and thought it prudent to remain out of sight in the surrounding forest. Believe me, Djagal isn't a timid man. However, he says these men were armed with military hardware.''

"Are you sure he's not telling you this because he thinks that's what you want to hear?" Katz inquired.

"He knows better than to lie to me," Rasul stated with a rather unpleasant smile. "The authorities wouldn't care much if a small-time smuggler washed up on shore. That sort of thing happens from time to time in Borneo. Djagal knows it can happen again.''

"Did he happen to notice where these men went?" Encizo persisted.

"Most of them left, but some of them are still at the cove with the boat," Rasul answered with a shrug. "Djagal is rather annoyed about this because he can't conduct any business as long as those blokes are there.''

"Then he won't mind if we pay them a visit and perhaps liberate the cove for him," Katz commented as he reached for his prosthesis and placed it in his lap. He rolled up the right sleeve of his bush shirt. "This Djagal isn't involved in drugs, prostitution or something like that?''

"Nothing of the sort," Rasul assured him. "He smuggles television sets, radios, that sort of thing from Java to Borneo and tobacco, yams, pepper and such crops grown here to Java. Restaurants buy them cheap that way. A lot of black-market merchandise and smuggling isn't terribly sinister. It just cheats the government out of some tax profits. Some of the big businesses might lose some money because the black market provides goods for a better price."

"Uh-huh," Encizo said dryly. He had seen enough smugglers in the past not to believe Rasul's description of the trade. "How do we get to this cove?"

"I'll guide you there," Rasul offered with a smile, "for another five hundred dollars."

"All right," Katz replied as he began to fit the prosthesis to the stump of his right arm. "You may as well make some more profits today. I just hope we have some good fortune of a different kind before the day is over."

17

The fishing boat was a large trawler with a wooden hull and wide decks. Two masts stood tall at the bow and stern, and the sails were down while the vessel was anchored in the cove. Four men were visible on the port side. A cabin blocked the view of the starboard side, but Phoenix Force assumed there were others on that side, as well. It was unlikely that anyone was in the cabins or in the cargo area because of the extreme heat and humidity.

Three men stood sentry on the beach by a group of wooden crates. They wore cotton work clothes and conical woven hats. One wore sandals, and the others were barefoot. Two of them carried krises in their belts, but none of the men on the beach or the vessel seemed to carry firearms. Of course, that only meant no guns were in view.

"You fellows stay awake," Amir Said whispered to Yakov Katzenelenbogen as he crouched beside him, hidden behind a dense wall of plants and palm trees. "Please?"

"That's why we got some sleep earlier," Katz replied. "Be careful out there."

Said nodded. He moved past a thick tree trunk where Gary Manning was stationed. The Canadian had assembled his H&K G-3 rifle with scope, and he knelt by the tree to use it as a post rest. A disc-shaped plastic object similar to a Frisbee lay on the ground by his left knee. Manning glanced up at Said and nodded.

Rasul had guided Phoenix Force and Said to the cove, and he had left as soon as he'd received payment for the chore. The commandos had observed the boat and men at the site and then quickly formed a plan. It was potentially very risky, and Said had agreed to take on the most dangerous job. He could not carry his H&K submachine gun or shoulder holster rig, but his Browning pistol was hidden under his shirt in the small of his back.

Said drew his parang and began to chop a path through the dense foliage. He saw movement among the branches of a nearby fruit tree and turned to see a manlike head and shoulders among the leaves. Said was startled and almost reached for his pistol. He knew McCarter was hidden somewhere in the mangrove, but he knew the commando would not be positioned so close to the others and he also doubted that McCarter would climb a tree, since the branches would offer precious little cover in a gun battle. Fleetingly he considered the possibility that the figure in the tree was an enemy lookout.

A moment later Said nearly laughed with relief. The face that looked down from the branches was framed by reddish-brown hair with streaks of white. Bright eyes peered from above a long, flat, drooping nose. It was a large proboscis monkey, about seventy-five centimeters long, not including its tail. The odd-looking primate is native only to Borneo. The monkey watched in fascination as Said hacked through the rain forest toward the beach.

Said finally emerged panting and successful from the dense foliage and stepped onto the sand. The three men by the crates had heard him chopping away at the vegetation. They were facing him when he finally appeared. Five other figures stood on the decks of the trawler. They all watched Said suspiciously as the ex-CIA agent approached.

"Allah's peace be with you," Said called out in Indonesian.

"Terima Kasih," the largest of the three men replied dryly as he stepped closer. "Thank you. What do you want?"

Said noticed the man had ignored the standard polite reply of a good Muslim and did not return his wish for Allah's blessing. These characters evidently had little interest in Islamic charity or good will.

"I need to return to Java, but I do not have money for transportation," Said explained. "I hoped I could come aboard your boat if you were headed for Java...."

"How did you know about our boat?" the man demanded. His hand rested lightly on the *ulu* handle of the kris in his belt.

"I picked some oranges from one of the fruit trees and saw it," Said replied innocently. "I thought you might be some of those men from the *Mérah Tentera* base in Bali...."

"Musuh ular" the man exclaimed, and yanked the kris from his belt.

Said jumped back and drew his parang in a fast fluid motion. The other figures on the beach and the decks of the boat responded to the shouted warning that Said was an "enemy snake." Said was vaguely aware of them as he concentrated on the man who was about to lunge, his kris extended.

The opponent executed a fast knife thrust. Said blocked the attack with his parang, steel clanging against steel. The kris fighter ducked low and attempted another thrust, but Said's machete was a cutting weapon rather than a stabbing blade. He swung his arm in a figure-8 pattern and brought the heavy blade down on his opponent's bowed head. The edge split the man's skull open with a single blow.

Another man on the beach drew his kris and rushed toward Said. Meanwhile the third man reached between two stacks of crates for an AK-47 assault rifle. The men on the boat scrambled around the decks. Two suddenly had weapons in hand. One of them aimed his M-16 at Said.

Gary Manning had been watching the boat for such signs of activity. He cooly centered the cross hairs of his scoped rifle and triggered his G-3. The burst of 7.62 mm slugs picked off the rifleman aboard the boat. He fell backward, allowing his M-16 rifle to clatter against a handrail and into the water. The man collapsed across the deck, his heart ruptured.

The man armed with the Kalashnikov crouched by the crates and tried to determine where the shots came from. He swung his rifle toward the surrounding trees, but could not decide where the sniper was hidden. He did not know that Katz had him in the sights of his own H&K subgun until the Israeli opened fire and drilled the terrorist in the stomach and solar plexus with three 9 mm parabellums. The AK-47 fell from the man's fingers as he clutched his wounded torso and crumpled to the deck.

Said once again found himself facing an opponent armed with a kris. He raised his parang to chest level and jerked his arm forward as if to deliver a cross-body cut. The terrorist ducked and weaved to avoid the stroke, then realized that Said's move was a feint. He lunged quickly to try to stab Said before the latter could follow up the bluff with whatever real attack he had in mind.

As he lunged, Said stepped smoothly forward to move behind his opponent. The ex-CIA agent whipped his parang low and slashed the man across the back of the knee.

The man cried out and fell to the ground, his leg bleeding heavily. Even so, the fanatic tried to push himself up to swing the kris at Said. He caught a blur of motion out of the corner of his eye just as he felt the sharp edge of the machete strike his neck. Said had been too sly and too quick for him. The man was already unconscious as his severed head rolled from the stump of his neck.

David McCarter fired a salvo of H&K submachine gun rounds at the handrail on the port side of the boat. Splinters erupted from the wooden barrier. Terrorists retreated from the rail and moved away from the stern. Katz fired another barrage of bullets at the bow to keep them from heading for the opposite end of the boat. Amir Said took advantage of this distraction to run to the cover of the crates. He discarded his bloodied parang and drew the 9 mm Browning from the small of his back, but held his fire.

While the enemy concentrated on the port side, they were unaware of a lone figure swimming silently below the surface of the cove to the starboard. Rafael Encizo held his breath as he breaststroked cleanly through the water. He had not brought air tanks or diving fins in his duffel bag. The only diving gear the Cuban frogman had was a diving mask. That was enough. He could see well enough despite the murky waters, and the distraction supplied by his teammates allowed him to gulp air into his lungs as he swam.

When he reached the bow, Encizo groped inside the rubber bag strapped to his chest. He removed a limpet mine with four spikes at its base and slammed it into the wooden hull to nail it into place. Then he gulped more air into his lungs and slid underwater once more. He made his way under the boat to the stern and waited for the bomb to go off.

The explosion rocked the vessel and tore a huge hole in the bow of the boat. The boat quickly began to shift as water poured into the gaping hole. Encizo descended again and swam away from the vessel with strong, efficient strokes.

Gary Manning emerged from the rain forest with the disc-shaped object in his hands. Between the sinking boat and the covering fire by Katz and McCarter, the enemy had their hands full. The demolitions experts calmly aimed the disc and hurled it at the boat. The plastic saucer sailed above the crates and lowered gracefully to the top of the cabin. The timer triggered the detonator to explode a small charge of CV-38. The blast tore planks loose from the cabin while presenting a minimum of risk to the terrorists on board.

The enemy was effectively trapped on the sinking vessel. One man appeared on the port side and fired a Beretta M-12 in a wild spray of bullets at the jungle. David McCarter nailed him with a burst of H&K slugs. Two other *Mérah Tentera* members jumped from the boat and splashed into the water. One man waded ashore, an AK-47 in his fists. He raised the rifle to his shoulder, aimed at the muzzle flash of Katz's subgun among the trees and squeezed the trigger.

He did not know the barrel was clogged with water.

The AK-47 exploded in his hands, and the chamber burst metal shards into his face like a hundred tiny steel darts. The man dropped the Kalashnikov, grabbed his shredded face and fell back into the water as his horrified comrade staggered on to shore.

The lone surviving terrorist raised his hands in surrender and stared at the trees. He gasped for breath and wondered if the mysterious attackers would take him alive or kill him on the spot. Amir Said stepped from behind the crates and pointed his pistol at him. The terrorist saw him and plunged breathlessly toward him.

Rafael Encizo emerged from the water behind the *Mérah Tentera* flunky. He pulled off his diving mask to clear his vision and stepped closer. The man was so intent on reaching Said that he did not notice Encizo. The Cuban swung a fist to the mastoid behind the terrorist's left ear. The man groaned and fell unconscious into his arms.

AMIR SAID KNELT by the senseless terrorist's feet and carefully sewed a small black metal button to a pant cuff. McCarter was positioned by the guy's head and watched for signs that the stooge might be regaining consciousness. An eyelash fluttered, so McCarter slammed his fist into the man's jaw to make sure he remained unconscious.

"Crude anesthetic," Gary Manning remarked, and shook his head.

"You reckon you could do better?" the Briton inquired.

Encizo returned once more from the water and pulled off his diving mask. He told the others he had searched the sunken boat in the cove and found two more dead terrorists, who had apparently been knocked out by the explosions and drowned in the cabins.

"So this fellow is the only survivor," Katz remarked as he blew cigarette smoke from his nostrils. "Our odds might be better if we managed to take two or more alive."

"Don't worry," Said assured him as he finished sewing the button on the man's cuff. "This little device is powered by an americium power battery, sort of a synthetic uranium. It'll keep sending signals for at least five months. The shell to the button is titanium. As long as he doesn't remove the button, we'll be able to track him with the receiver.''

"I still think we ought to try interrogating this bastard," McCarter declared. "For all we know, he'll just head for the nearest village and lie low for a while. Hell, he may not even know where the enemy base is."

"True," Katz agreed as he dropped his half-smoked Camel to the ground and crushed it under a boot. "But Mr. Jones isn't here, so he can't administer scopolamine. Terrorists don't generally give information just because you offer them a deal or threaten them. Trying to beat information out of him is out of the question. It probably wouldn't work, anyway."

"Well, this fella was willing to surrender," McCarter reminded the Israeli. "Maybe he wouldn't be so tough to break."

"Maybe," Katz allowed. "But we can't try other methods and then use the tracker. Not enough time to do that, anyway. Let's just hope this works."

"They say hope springs eternal," Manning commented. "I just wish I believed it."

"I'd say a little optimism isn't out of place," Encizo stated with a smile. "Our first gamble to try to catch up with the terrorists by using Amir's connections here in Borneo paid off. Maybe we're on a winning streak."

"That'd be nice," Katz replied. "Okay. Let's get out of here and let this man wake up on his own. I hope he doesn't suffer from amnesia after being punched in the head."

"I thought that only happened in the movies and on television," McCarter said. "On TV people get amnesia more often than the flu."

"Yeah," Manning agreed.

"Let's continue this discussion elsewhere," Katz urged.

They left the cove and moved deep into the jungle. Amir Said retrieved his duffel bag, which contained the receiver unit for the tracking device. A small single dot appeared on the screen. After a few minutes, it began to move, slowly at first. Said announced that the man they had tagged was on his feet and probably checking his fellow terrorists at the cove to see if any of them were alive.

"Now he's headed north," Said declared. "The range on this tracker is about two miles. No way we'll lose the man unless he discovers the button. I've used these things before, and it's pretty rare for a subject to realize he's been tagged. The times it's happened, the subject was smarter than this slimy terrorist seems to be."

"It's hard to say how smart he might be," Manning remarked. "We didn't even talk to him."

"That's true," Encizo admitted. "But I doubt he's very bright, or he wouldn't be a terrorist in the first place."

"Regardless of how intelligent he might be," Katz mused as he reached inside his own duffel bag, "lets hope he's not especially observant or suspicious. He may wonder why he was left alive, but he'll probably assume that was an accident, and he'll think we believed all the terrorists were killed. We left him for dead. Makes sense...if one doesn't question it too much."

"More likely he'll wonder who the hell attacked the boat and why," McCarter said grimly. "If we can trust what we've learned so far, these blokes who arrived on the trawler probably don't know the base in Bali was hit, unless the colonel and the Djarios brothers saw fit to share that information with them."

"If they knew smugglers use the cove, he may assume the attack was by local gangsters upset about competition in the area," Encizo said. "In fact, because we didn't take any prisoners and overlooked the sole survivor, even the leaders of *Mérah Tentera* may not be too suspicious."

"I would be," Katz stated. "We'd better assume the colonel will consider every possibility. He's done a pretty good job of that so far. He's made mistakes, but not many. He'll probably have our friend searched for bugs when and *if* he arrives at the base."

"If he doesn't lead us to the base, I'm going to be damned disappointed," McCarter muttered.

"You won't be the only one!" Manning agreed.

Katz removed a powerful compact transceiver from his bag, pulled up the antenna and adjusted it to Major Tukarno's frequency. The PMB officer and forty Police Mobile Brigade troops waited at a base at the island of Laut, off the coast of Borneo. Katz pressed the transmit button and spoke into the handset.

"Eagle One, this is Eagle Two," he declared. "Do you read me? Over."

"Eagle One here," Tukarno's voice replied on the radio. "I read you, Eagle Two. Please report. Over."

"Some success so far," Katz answered. "If all goes well, we should have more good news."

"We'll eagerly await your next broadcast," Tukarno said. "However, that chap at the hospital has been trying to contact you. Should I give him a message?"

"No," Katz replied. "In fact, expect the next transmission to be on the other prearranged frequency in case that chap tries to eavesdrop. I'll contact you when I know more."

"Allah be with you," Tukarno said, and ended transmission.

"The chap at the hospital could be Mr. Jones," McCarter remarked.

"No," Katz assured him. "Tukarno used the term 'chap' on purpose. He was referring to Chappell, that CIA snoop. The Company and NSA are probably trying to monitor radio broadcasts to try to locate us. We don't need them here. They won't be any help to us in the field, and they may ruin the mission if they get in the way now."

"That's all we need," Encizo growled. "A Bay of Pigs, Indonesian-style."

"Unfortunately they'll find us eventually," Katz warned the others. "That means we're running out of time. If our unsuspecting ally fails to lead us to the enemy headquarters, this operation could go down the tubes."

"It's bad enough when you have to worry about the enemy," Manning complained. "It's worse when you have to watch out for the people who are supposed to be on your side."

"The signal is still moving north," Said announced as he examined the screen. "We don't want him to get too much of a head start if we want to catch up with him."

"Right," Katz agreed as he returned the radio to his duffel bag. "Well, gentlemen. It seems we get to spend more time hiking through the lovely green mangroves and rain forests of Borneo."

"That's one thing about this job," McCarter commented. "Gets you out of the house for a bit of exercise."

18

Borneo is the third largest island in the world. Greenland and New Guinea have first and second place; although larger, Australia is a continent. Borneo covers an area of approximately 750,000 square kilometers, yet Borneo's total population is about nine million. The island is larger than the state of Texas, and has roughly half the population of the Lone Star State.

As Phoenix Force struggled through the tropical rain forests, it did not seem surprising to them that so much of the island's formidable territory was uninhabited. Among his many accomplishments, Yakov Katzenelenbogen was knowledgeable in archaeology, and he recalled bits and pieces of Borneo's history. The Sumatra-based kingdom of Sri Vijaya had extended Indian influence and culture to the west coast of Borneo around 400 A.D. The Majapahit Empire of Java gained control of southern Borneo in the fourteenth century, and by the sixteenth century, the Brunei sultanate ruled northern Borneo and the Sulu Archipelago, as well. The budding empire of Southeast Asia was now the Delaware-size state of Brunei. What the tiny nation of Brunei lacks in territory, it compensates for in great wealth, thanks to its substantial reserves of petroleum and natural gas. On average, the citizens of Brunei earn an income thirty-eight times greater than that of their Indonesian neighbors in the Kalimantan portion of Borneo and fourteen times more than the Malaysian populations in the northern states of Sabah and Sarawak.

During the seventeenth and nineteenth centuries, the British and the Dutch took an interest in Borneo. They were largely concerned with the pepper trade. Chinese settlers discovered gold in western Borneo, so the Dutch took over their former settlements in 1854. The British ruled the northern portion, and the Dutch controlled southern Borneo until 1949, yet the European colonies largely remained in the coastal areas. The interior of Borneo remained much the same as it had been when the island belonged only to the Dayaks and the magnificent wildlife that still dominates much of its topography.

The chattering of a troop of macaque monkeys in nearby trees announced the approach of the four Phoenix commandos and Amir Said. Smaller than the proboscis monkey, the diminutive primates were easily alarmed by the human intruders. They leaped from branch to branch and clustered together for comfort. When the group of men continued on their way without presenting any threat, the monkeys relaxed and returned to their normal activities once more.

The trek through the dense bush was long and difficult. Said's receiver unit kept them informed of the progress of their helpful terrorist. Their quarry continued to move deeper inland, into the island's interior. The peaks of small mountains were barely visible above the treetops.

"He's about a mile ahead of us and seems to be headed toward the mountains," Said estimated as he studied the screen on his device.

"All right," Katz declared, his H&K subgun cradled by his prosthesis. "Remember the detectors they had at the base in Bali. They'll probably have something like that here. Keep an eye out for anything of that sort. They may have their camp at the mountains."

"Yeah," Manning agreed. "That would be a natural choice. The mountains would give them cover on at least one side. They could be disguised as a mining operation or something that would look innocent to most observers."

"Except there isn't much mining done in this area," Said explained. "Mother Nature or Allah or whatever gave Brunei the best mineral deposits in Borneo, as well as the oil and natural gas. The gold in the west was mined out by the Dutch and the Chinese nearly a century ago, but it hasn't run out in Brunei. Neither have the copper and iron. The Malaysian states do most of the mining for tin, manganese, bauxite, that sort of thing."

"Well, we don't know anything for sure until we get close enough to see for ourselves." McCarter sighed. "I sure as hell hope this it it. That little bastard may just plan to camp by the mountains tonight."

Encizo took a long drink of water and a canteen and wiped his dripping forehead. "It will be dark soon. How dangerous is it here at night?"

"There aren't any cannibals or headhunters running around," Said answered. "I doubt you'd even find them in New Guinea anymore. There are tigers in Bali and Sumatra, but not in Borneo. Orangutans live here, but they're only dangerous killers in Edgar Allan Poe's short story. The honey bears and pythons aren't much of a threat to humans, and we're not close enough to the river to worry about crocodiles. The most dangerous wildlife in Borneo is probably certain species of poisonous snakes."

"If you don't include terrorists," Manning added.

"Or us," McCarter said with a wolfish grin.

"Let's keep moving," Katz instructed. "Just stay alert. There are only five of us, and we have no idea how many

Mérah Tentera terrorists might be at the base. *If* we find it.''

THE PHOENIX FORCE commander's concern that they might not locate the enemy lair was dispelled three hours later. Between the stalks of great thistles and the trunks of ironwood trees, the commandos peered at the base of the mountains. A dirt path had been laboriously cleared around the dark rock walls. Two large three-ton trucks were parked on the improvised road. The vehicles were a surprising feature to the intruders, since it hardly seemed possible that they could be used in the thick tropical vegetation. The path extended around the foot of the mountains, which suggested there was ample clearing beyond to drive to the river and possibly escape by boats or raft if necessary. Two armed figures stood guard by the trucks.

Several ladders were placed along the rock walls, leading to stone ridges and numerous caves. Steady pale light glowed from inside the caves—electric light powered by generators. Columns of black smoke rose from holes in stone that acted as chimney flues. The elaborate setup startled Phoenix Force. They were not sure what they would find when they located the terrorist base, but they certainly did not expect to discover the *Mérah Tentera* living in such comfort in the side of a mountain.

Phoenix Force and Amir Said watched the site for almost half an hour. They spotted more false ferns among the colorful orchids and rhododendrons that flanked the mountains. This time the commando unit stayed far enough from the detection devices to avoid triggering the enemy alarm system.

Katz gestured for the others to follow. He led them away from the terrorist base and deeper into the jungle. When they were half a kilometer from the site, Katz quietly addressed the others.

"Those caves could box the terrorists in rather nicely if we handle this properly," he remarked as he reached inside his bag for his transceiver.

"I can't believe they managed to dig out those caves just to use for their base," Manning remarked. "A project like that would take at least a year, even if they used heavy machinery and demolitions."

"They didn't build the dwellings," Said declared. "Those have been there for centuries. Some of the Dayak tribes used to live in caves in a sort of community housing system. The caves are probably natural. The aboriginals probably enlarged them with stone tools and connected them with tunnels. It was good protection against warring tribes in the old days. Climb up ladders and ropes to the caves and pull them up so the enemies can't follow. Then you throw rocks and spears down on your attackers."

"Sort of like castle walls without the castle," McCarter mused.

"That's the idea," Said confirmed. "Once upon a time, it was an effective defense. As it is, they've got good cover among the rocks and an elevated position to fire down at invading forces. It'll still work against most types of attacks they'd be apt to encounter."

"It's going to cause us serious problems if the five of us have to handle this base on our own," Encizo remarked. "We'd better get Turkano and the PMB to back us up."

"Yes," Katz answered as he pulled up the antenna to his transceiver and pressed down the transmit button. He pushed a latch on the handset and adjusted the frequency dial. "Since CIA and NSA and God knows who else may be scanning radio broadcasts, I've set this on a homing signal. When Tukarno gets it, he'll know to load up his men in the Chinooks and leave immediately. The signal will guide him here.''

"How long will it take them to get here?" Said wondered aloud.

"Troops are on standby," McCarter replied, drawing from his own experience with the SAS. "They might be a bit relaxed since our last broadcast, but Tukarno is a good officer. He'll be on their butts enough to make sure they're ready and alert. Shouldn't take more than two to five minutes to load up the men and weapons. Probably less if the PMB is as efficient as they've seemed to be so far. Once they get those Chinooks airborne, I reckon they can be here in ten minutes, unless they have trouble tracking the signal.''

"But they may have trouble locating the site from the air even if they follow the signal well enough," Encizo remarked. "Too bad you couldn't broadcast verbally.''

"The terrorists have radio communications, too," Katz stated. "They'd be fools if they didn't, and we wouldn't have had to go through this much trouble if they were fools. If they monitor radio wavelengths, they'll be tipped off if they hear a broadcast that sounds the least bit suspicious whether I make it in English or Amir speaks in Indonesian. Since none of us guessed the terrorists might be using mountainside caves for their base, I don't know how we could hint at that and indirectly tell Tukarno without informing the enemy, as well.''

"And they're close enough they'd certainly hear the broadcast," Said agreed. "An ordinary CB radio could pick up from this distance. They may even be suspicious when they hear the constant buzz of the homing signal.''

"I imagine they will be," Katz answered. "Especially since our little friend with the tracking tag button is in there and no doubt told them what happened at the cove . . . or at least as much as he knows. The colonel and the Djarios brothers will have this figured out any moment now if they haven't already."

"Hell," Manning rasped. "They could pull out of here and be on the river by the time Tukarno and the others arrive."

"That's why we have to head back right now," Katz replied. "If they try to pull out, we'll have to stall them and hold them off until Tukarno and the Chinooks arrive. If we're extremely lucky, they'll be holed up in the caves, trying to make up their minds, until reinforcements get here. Then we can signal Tukarno with a flare as soon as we hear the Chinooks."

"And if we're not lucky?" Said asked grimly. "Which seems to be more likely, the way this mission has gone so far."

"Then the PMB will certainly notice all the gunfire and explosions near the mountains," Katz answered grimly. "They'll see it from the air and have no trouble determining which side the enemy is, based on sheer numbers."

"And you think we can hold them off for ten minutes or longer?" Said rolled his eyes toward the black night above. "I used to think I had some dangerous assignments when I was with the Company, but CIA was never anything like this."

"Thank God," Encizo said with a smile.

"It is dangerous," Katz admitted. "Of course, this mission has been very dangerous from the beginning. That's why Jones is in the hospital and a number of Police Mobile Brigade troops are dead or injured. Not to mention all the unarmed and untrained innocent civilians who have also been victims of the *Mérah Tentera*."

"I know," Said replied, and shook his head. "Let's go back and give the old roulette wheel one more spin. Seems to me we've cheated death quite a few times already. I don't know if our luck will hold out much longer."

"You don't count on luck," McCarter declared. "You rely on your training, experience and instincts. When the battle is raging, that's what you've got. Your skills and reflexes against the other bloke's. Think of it as the ultimate contest."

"You always have," Manning retorted.

"I'm still alive, mate," the Briton reminded him with a grin. "So are you. Don't tell me you don't look at this much the same way I do, Miller. You wouldn't still be doing this sort of thing if you didn't like the challenge and the danger, as well as the importance of doing a vital job to defend innocent folks and protect the interests of the United States and the rest of the so-called civilized world."

19

Munap Djarios was furious. It was a truly crude and uncouth insult he bellowed into the face of the lone survivor from the attack on the cove before yelling at him, "You've led them to us!"

Munap's big fist crashed into the man's face and sent him smashing into a stone wall. The unlucky terrorist slumped to the floor of the cave, his mouth bleeding and his eyes dazed. Munap prepared to kick him, too, but Hasan held him back.

Colonel Qui barely noticed Munap's angry treatment of the *Mérah Tentera* stooge. The Vietnamese officer did not care about the man one way or the other. He gripped the black metal button in his fist. Qui had discovered it when he searched the fool for miniature microphones and tracking devices. He was not certain how the button worked, but he recognized it for what it was.

"He thought smugglers had attacked the boat at the cove," Hasan said in defense of the battered man. "After all, they just left him for dead. You can't blame him for thinking they had overlooked him...."

"Thinking isn't his strong point," Qui said grimly, but his voice was soft as he considered his next move. "I want sentries posted up high on the mountain and machine guns stationed at each cave to cell entrances. If a large military force is closing in, I want to know about it before they can get within range.''

"Range of what?'' Munap demanded. "Rifles? Grenade launchers? Mortars? They could be five kilometers away and blow these caves to pieces.''

"I was in a real war,'' Qui replied. "Remember? I'm aware of that far better than you are, Munap.''

A *Mérah Tentera* follower named Gunawan appeared at a tunnel that connected the colonel's temporary headquarters with the communications center of the Borneo base. Gunawan was the group's top radio operator. He seemed worried as he moved through the tunnel. The sight of the the lone survivor of the cove incident sprawled on the floor of the cave with half his teeth knocked out did nothing to ease his fears.

"I was told to report any suspicious radio broadcasts....'' he began awkwardly.

"What is it?'' Qui demanded, and fixed a hard stare on Gunawan's face.

"It may be nothing,'' the radioman began. "But there is a strange continuous buzzing sound on one frequency. It may be a malfunction in a radio station or some other radio transmitter, but the sender would probably realize this and either discontinue broadcast until the problem is corrected or change to another frequency.''

"It may be static,'' Hasan suggested.

"No,'' Gunawan replied. "This isn't ordinary static. It's high-pitched and seems almost deliberate. There are no mingled voices on the frequency distorted by the noise or the usual crackle of static.''

"It's a radio beacon,'' Qui declared. "Someone is sending a message to serve as a tracking device for others to find their way here.''

"That may be correct," Gunawan said reluctantly. "But there may be another explanation, Colonel."

"I'm afraid not," Hasan replied grimly. "All the evidence suggests the enemy is closing in on us."

"What are we going to do?" Gunawan asked as he glanced from Hasan to Colonel Qui.

The Vietnamese officer had turned to stare at his improvised altar on the steamer trunk by his cot. A light bulb glowed above the incense burners and small trays where offerings were made to Buddha. Qui had no time to pray and doubted he would receive divine guidance. Conventional wisdom based on his military career would have to do.

"I've already given suggestions about our defenses," Qui said. "In addition, I think we should prepare the vehicles to leave as soon as possible and send a detachment of men into the rain forest to deal with the enemies already here."

"What do you mean?" Munap inquired with a frown.

"If enough forces were here to launch an attack now," Qui began, "they would have done so. They would not have to signal for reinforcements. That means there must be a fairly small group of opponents in the jungle, beyond the range of the heat and motion detectors. They're doing basic reconnaissance, but they cannot radio intelligence to the reinforcements because they realize we'd pick it up on our radios, as well."

"So we hunt them down and kill them," Hasan said with a puzzled expression. "What will that accomplish if others are coming in greater numbers?"

"First," Qui said, annoyed by the question because he considered the answer obvious, "they won't be able to give intelligence information and details about our base to the main force when it arrives. Second, and most important, if we can take them out now, we may be able to locate the radio transmitter sending the homing signal and shut it down before the reinforcements arrive."

"The enemy will still have a general idea where our base is," Hasan insisted.

"But this can delay them long enough to allow us to get a decent head start when we flee," Qui explained patiently. "If we leave, the reconnaissance unit will follow us and continue to transmit their homing signal. If they're dead, they cannot reveal any information or send radio signals."

"Agreed," Hasan said grimly. He buckled his gun belt with holstered pistol around his waist and slung his *penjut* across a shoulder. "I'll see to it, Colonel."

"Take that idiot with you," Qui said, and pointed at the dazed man who was trying to rise from the floor of the cave. "He can be one of the men sent to find the enemy scouts. Put him at point. If any of our comrades have to die, he deserves to be one of them."

"You're very cavalier with the lives of Indonesians," Munap remarked. The big man had lost his temper with the fellow when he returned from the cove, but Munap did not believe the man should die for his carelessness.

Qui looked at Gunawan and told him to return to the radio and continue monitoring broadcasts. Gunawan reentered the tunnel, and Qui glared at Munap.

"You know better than to talk in such a manner in front of the others," the Vietnamese officer hissed. "As for sacrificing lives, that's part of the burden of command. Do you want to be a leader, Munap? Those hard responsibilities are part of it."

"You and Hasan are the leaders here," Munap replied with disgust. "You can have your 'responsibilities,' but other men shed their blood for your decisions."

"You're my brother," Hasan told him. "We've always been together and we always will be."

"If you want to die together, that's up to you," Qui declared as he glared at the Djarios brothers. "If you want to live, you'll listen to me."

Hasan and Munap exchanged glances. They knew Qui was the real professional, and the colonel had already demonstrated his ability to stay alive. He was ruthless and callous, but he knew how to survive. The Djarios brothers realized their best chance to survive was to stay with Colonel Qui.

"We're listening," Hasan told him.

WHEN PHOENIX FORCE and Amir Said returned to the site of the enemy base, they realized that something had happened. The increased activity around the cave dwellings showed that the terrorists had figured out that they were about to be besieged. Additional sentries were posted along the rock walls, and the barrels of mounted machine guns jutted from the mouths of caves. Several men were posted by the trucks. About a dozen more were headed into the jungle, weapons held at the ready and night-vision goggles strapped to their heads.

"*Cristo,*" Rafael Encizo hissed under his breath. "They're hunting us."

"Yeah," Manning whispered, "but they made a mistake. Notice the goggles? They're using the old infrared models."

"So?" Said remarked tensely. "They can still see in the dark better than we can."

"Maybe not for long," Katz replied. "Don't use your guns unless you have to. We can't afford to waste ammo, and we can't match the firepower of those mounted machine guns."

"The terrorists have been using weapons they probably stole from military installations or brought from black market sources here in Indonesia," Said commented. "That means the machine guns are probably .30-caliber Madsen Mark II light machine guns manufactured here for the military."

"The Indonesian version of the Danish model," Manning added.

"Well, la-dee-dah," McCarter rasped with annoyance. "We've got gun-toting problems headed straight for us."

"Right," Katz agreed. "You come with me, Collins. We're going to try to circle around to cover the back door and their driveway. The rest of you get the front."

"Thanks," Encizo said dryly.

The terrorist gunmen advanced into the bush. Most were carrying M-12 submachine guns, short-range weapons with plenty of firepower and a rapid cyclic rate. A few carried assault rifles. They fanned out in an expanding horseshoe and scanned the foliage with their headsets.

One *Mérah Tentera* gunman pushed his way through a cluster of large ferns and elephant grass. He thought he glimpsed movement among some ironwood trees and swung his Beretta subgun toward the thick tree trunks. Some leaves stirred in the gentle night breeze, and the terrorist grunted, not sure whether he was relieved or disappointed that he had not spotted one of the invaders.

Encizo waited on all fours, his body covered by the big floppy leaves, as the terrorist passed scant centimeters from his position without detecting him. By remaining still and breathing shallowly and silently through his open mouth, he was able to stifle even the sound of air passing through his nostrils.

Just as the terrorist started to turn, Encizo suddenly sprang up from the ferns. He grabbed the man from behind, wrapping his left arm around his neck and throat. With the big Muela Bowie in his right hand, he plunged seven centimeters of sharp molybdenum-vanadium steel into his opponent's left kidney. Encizo yanked the blade free and heard the familiar sickly sucking sound as it cleared flesh. He shifted his left arm to cover the man's mouth with his hand and sliced his throat open with the next stroke.

Another terrorist thrashed through the foliage to reach his comrade. He saw Encizo holding the first *Mérah Tentera* man from behind, but he didn't know the man was already dead. The second terrorist held his fire as he closed in.

Rafael Encizo turned sharply and shoved the dead man into his lunging opponent. The second gunman was knocked backward. Encizo hissed, furious with himself. He should have been more patient and remained hidden instead of jumping the first guy. Too late now.

He rushed his surprised attacker and swiftly slashed the Bowie across the back of the man's fist to sever the tendons. The man's useless fingers popped open around the pistol grip of the M-12 chopper. Encizo's other arm swung at the wrist above the front grips of the subgun striking the weapon from the man's grasp.

The terrorist bent his right arm and hooked a front-elbow smash to the side of Encizo's face. The blow stunned the commando, who staggered two steps back as his opponent drew a kris from his belt with his good left hand. The terrorist held the knife in an icepick grip.

"Tolong!" the man shouted as he attacked Encizo.

The Cuban was familiar with many styles of Asian knife fighting. A Westerner wielding a knife with an overhand icepick grip usually does not know how to fight with a blade, and the attack will be clumsy and choppy, fairly easy for an experienced knifeman to deal with. However, many Asian styles use this grip to slash and stab in a manner similar to the punches and chops of a fighter's martial-arts training.

Pentjak-silat again, Encizo realized. He wished he knew more about the Indonesian combat forms, but there was little he could do for the moment. Encizo would simply have to rely on his own skill and hope his opponent was as unfamiliar with *his* style.

The terrorist raised the kris high, as if to strike, then swung a kick for Encizo's groin. The Cuban expected the move; it was a standard technique for streetfighters throughout the world. He presented his thigh swiftly, protecting his privates. The kick stung, but his thick leg muscles absorbed the blow.

Then the knifeman swung his arm as if to throw a left hook to slash Encizo with the blade. The Cuban parried the attack with a clang of steel, and he decisively slammed his free arm under his opponent's extended forearm to drive the armed fist upward. The man's arm also rose, and Encizo quickly followed up with a powerful thrust of his Bowie into the exposed armpit.

The man screamed as the steel drove home. He tried to slash at Encizo, but his arm would not respond. The Cuban extracted the blade from his opponent's body and shoved him to the ground. He kicked him under the jaw to keep him down for a while, but the man was already in shock and hemorrhaging seriously. He would die without regaining consciousness.

Another *Mérah Tentera* thug had heard the scream and headed toward the sound. He saw two struggling figures among the ferns and tall grass, but he could not tell which was a comrade and which the enemy. He was not accustomed to the infrared goggles, which seemed to be more trouble than they were worth. Nothing looked right to his eyes. Colors were different, and shapes were bathed in a sickly glow.

"Tolong," a voice whispered from a tree trunk.

The man turned, expecting to see a colleague. Amir Said stepped from behind the ironwood trunk and swung his parang with both fists wrapped around the handle. The terrorist gasped and raised his M-16 to ward off the blow. The machete blade struck forcibly and knocked the rifle from his hands.

The man jumped back and whipped out a *tjabang*. An iron truncheon with hooked tines at each side of the metal shaft, it is similar to the *sai* used in some styles of Okinawan karate. The center blade is not sharp, but the end is pointed and can puncture bamboo armor. Said was not wearing armor. Neither was his opponent. He stepped forward and swung the parang blade at the terrorist's wrist in an effort to disarm him.

The *tjabang* moved swiftly to block Said's blade, which struck the center shaft harmlessly. The man turned the *tjabang* to trap the machete between the shaft and a tine hook. Then he suddenly pulled hard and swung a kick to Said's arms, flipping the machete out of Said's hand and into the bush.

The fanatic slashed the *tjabang* in a cross-body stroke intended for Said's skull. Said stepped forward and chopped both hands across his forearm to block the attack. He swiftly grabbed the man's wrist with one hand and clawed at the terrorist's face with his other hand. The goggles protected the man's eyes, but Said's fingernails raked the man's cheeks and his lower face.

As he did so, Said crooked a leg behind his opponent's ankle and shoved one hand against the terrorist's face while continuing to hold the man's wrist to keep the truncheon at bay. Struggling mightily but overcome, the *Mérah Tentera* man tripped and fell. Said kicked him sharply in the head and wrenched the *tjabang* from his grasp. He descended on his dazed foe unhesitantly and drove the point of his own weapon deep into the fallen man's heart.

The other terrorists heard the sounds of the battle in the bush and turned to follow when a small object landed on the ground just a few kilometers away from them. They turned toward the sound as a magnesium flare burst into brilliant white light. The infrared system intensified it to a blinding degree. They shrieked as it seemed to sear through their eyeballs. One man threw down his rifle to claw his goggles off, afraid the rig had somehow exploded and driven glass shards into his eyes.

That's what you get for not using the Starlite system, Gary Manning thought as he emerged from the bushes and headed toward the helpless pair. He stayed alert to his surroundings, aware that other opponents may have spotted the flare. Of course, if they got a good look, they would also be blind or at least partially unable to see. Indeed, a third terrorist stumbled toward him, a subgun in one hand and the other pawing at his goggles as if somehow this would help him to see.

Manning was almost reluctant to open fire on him, but the man was still armed and had a general idea of where the Canadian was. The Canadian triggered a 3-round burst that lifted the man off his feet and dumped him lifeless to the ground. The other terrorists heard the gunfire, but could not see if it had been done by friend or foe. The guy who still held his weapon swung it toward Manning but held his fire.

The Canadian marched forward, gripping his own G-3 rifle by the barrel. Swinging it like a baseball bat, he smartly clubbed the gun from his opponent. The blinded fanatic gasped and tried to grab for him. Manning easily dodged him and delivered a finishing butt-stroke to the side of the man's neck. As he collapsed unconscious, his remaining colleague's vision began to clear.

With a bestial roar the last terrorist launched himself at Manning and grabbed the frame of the rifle with both hands. The Canadian warrior pulled hard, folded a leg and dropped to the ground. The terrorist was hauled forward to meet Manning's boot. The Canadian planted his foot in the man's abdomen and straightened his leg to send him flying head-over-heels in a judo circle-throw.

Manning started to get up when a volley of automatic fire suddenly sprayed the surrounding vegetation. Bullets struck trees and plants around him. Dirt sprang up from the ground in tiny geysers less than a meter away. He dived behind an ironwood tree. A scream of pain indicated that the terrorist he had previously struggled with had not managed to do likewise.

The intensity of the enemy firepower and its indiscriminate spray of bullets was coming from the light machine guns set up at the caves. Obviously lookouts had spotted the flare and rifle fire in the rain forest. They had decided to open up with the Madsen death machines even if doing so meant they might blast their own people in the process.

Manning stayed low behind the tree trunk and waited for the shooting to subside. It was impossible to say what the besieged terrorists might use next. Manning wondered what sort of arsenal they had. Grenades, to be sure. Even if they could not steal military grenades, such explosives are not difficult to improvise. From their elevated position on the rock walls, they could hurl grenades a good distance into the rain forest. It was quite likely they had launchers and perhaps mortars.

"Son of a bitch," Manning rasped as he remained pinned down by machine gun fire. "Where the hell is Tukarno with the flying cavalry?"

20

As the machine gun fire continued to scatter into the surrounding rain forest, only three of the *Mérah Tentera* manhunters managed to escape its range to the jungle nearest the rear of the mountain fortress. The others had either been taken out by the enemy or cut down by "friendly fire" from the caves.

Angry and frightened by the barrage, the trio had almost forgotten the men they had been sent to deal with. They were working their way farther away from the line of fire when they suddenly halted. A manlike shape lay on the ground, half-covered by ferns and tall grass. Now that they had removed their infrared goggles, they discovered the night-vision devices boiled their eyes in brilliant light. They could not see the shape clearly in the dark, but it appeared to be the prone figure of a man.

They did not intend to take any chances. All three men opened fire. Bullets ripped into fabric and spun the shape over to reveal a jacket wrapped around over a bush that had been pulled roughly into a hunched posture, the top section pinned to the ground by a knife. The sleeve had been stuffed with a bent tree branch and bundles of leaves and elephant grass hastily ripped up from the ground.

In the second that it took to realize they had been tricked, two Heckler & Koch submachine guns opened fire on them. Yakov Katzenelenbogen and David McCarter blasted them with more than a dozen 9 mm slugs. The three collapsed in a twitching heap.

"They ruined my jacket," McCarter complained, looking at the shredded garment.

"At least you weren't wearing it at the time," Katz replied. He gazed at the steady streams of machine gun fire that streaked from the caves at the rain forest. "I hope to God the others found cover in time."

"What are we going to do now, Yakov?" McCarter inquired, tense with concern for his fellow commandos and Amir Said.

"We keep moving to the rear of the mountain. From this angle there's nothing we can do except get ourselves killed. The terrorists probably have escape tunnels back there. Besides keeping the enemy from getting away, we may be able to use those tunnels to hit them from a direction they aren't expecting...."

A sudden thunderous roar of mighty rotor blades chopping the heavy night air interrupted Katz. Treetops swayed violently as the giant metal hull of the sausage-shaped helicopter appeared above the trees. It hovered there like a monstrous beast from a nightmare realm.

The huge Chinook shifted in the air and pointed its blunt snout at the caves. Its machine gun turrets erupted tracer rounds that streaked toward the caves like jets of flame from the jaws of a massive flying dragon.

The barrage raked the rock walls and caves. Terrorist corpses tumbled from stony ridges to fall ten or more meters below to the ground. The whines of ricochets against stone were barely audible above the constant snarl of the chopper's guns. Some of the bullets entered caves and pinged on the inside rock walls before embedding themselves in human flesh.

"Major Tukarno didn't let us down," McCarter remarked cheerfully as he watched.

"Let's make sure we hold up our end as well," Katz replied.

They moved to the other side of the mountain. The rough dirt road extended into the distance, following a pathway painstakingly hacked through the jungle. It was not much of a clearing, and getting a vehicle through it would be difficult. In fact, it seemed unlikely that anything as large as a three-ton truck would be able to get through the narrow clearing unless it could plow through the thick tangle of foliage that had grown since the path was last cut. Vegetation grows rapidly in Borneo and after a few days it can already begin to compensate for man's efforts to clear it.

"Well, fancy that," the British ace commented when he saw two Land Rovers parked by some boulders. "Additional transportation."

Katz nodded. The sturdy vehicles were equipped with roll bars, reinforced tires and battering rams built into their front fenders. The British military machines could bully their way through anything short of a brick wall. The Rovers would have a far better chance of getting through the jungle than the trucks.

"Interesting that these are segregated from the other vehicles," Katz observed. "I have a strong suspicion why someone decided to do this."

"Someone is going to be bloody disappointed before the night's through," McCarter added with a wide grin that would have done justice to a hungry tiger shark.

THE CHINOOK effectively pinned down the terrorists and diverted their attention away from Manning, Encizo and Said. The big Canadian took advantage of this to search the area for his companions. He was relieved to find the Cuban warrior alive and uninjured, aside from a bruise on his left cheek. Manning failed to locate Amir Said, and Encizo didn't know what had happened to the ex-CIA agent, either.

"I hope he didn't catch a bullet when those bastards opened up with the machine guns," the Cuban said grimly.

"It was like a monsoon of bullets," Manning added, very much aware that he himself had barely reached cover in time to avoid being chopped to bits by it.

The terrorists at the caves tried to redirect their Madsen Mark II chatterguns to point up at the Chinook. This was awkward for them, and the steady firepower the gunship returned made the task even more difficult. On the ground the terrorists beside the trucks had been overlooked by the PMB chopper. Some of them climbed into the back of a rig and emerged with an object that resembled a big chunk of steel pipe set on a metal brace.

"Damn it," Manning cursed. "They've got a mortar. If they fire a shell and hit the Chinook, they can blow it out of the sky with a single HE shell."

"Like hell they will," Encizo replied as he moved toward the mountains. "Cover me, Gary."

The Cuban had retrieved his H&K subgun and used the barrel and frame to worry his way through the tangle of vines and bushes. Manning followed, his G-3 clenched in his fists. Encizo got as close as he dared without exposing himself to the terrorists. He dropped to his belly. Two of the men had ducked beside the rear of the truck with their weapons. One of them was feeding a shell into the wide bore of the mortar.

Encizo immediately aimed his MP-5 and opened fire. The pair staggered from the impact, their arms whirling in the air as they tried to keep their balance, scarlet spiders spreading over their shirtfronts. Encizo watched them fall and caught sight of another terrorist on his belly beneath the truck. He was aiming a rifle straight at Encizo.

Gary Manning had also noticed the rifleman. He centered the cross hairs of the G-3 scope on the would-be sniper's face and squeezed the trigger. A trio of 7.62 mm rounds tore the man's skull apart. The corpse slumped under the vehicle, a grisly warning to others.

Another pair of hands seized the mortar and dragged it behind the truck. Encizo expected this. The terrorists had forgotten about their other attackers in the forest and they were becoming careless. The Chinook seemed to present the major threat to their fortress. They would take greater pains to avoid presenting themselves as targets in future.

Encizo had already pulled the pin from an M-26 fragmentation grenade. He smoothly lobbed it overhand and watched it hit the ground and roll under the truck near the decapitated corpse. Encizo covered his head with his arms a second before it exploded. The blast tipped the truck over on its side, crushing the men preparing to use the mortar.

Manning prepared another disc-shaped explosive, this time loaded with a C-4 charge instead of the less powerful CV-38 explosives. He pushed aside some bushes with the barrel of his G-3 rifle and tossed the plastic saucer through the clearing. It spun through the air to descend gracefully among the trucks at the base of the mountain.

The tremendous blast blew apart the vehicles, bursting fuel tanks and igniting gasoline. Flames and fuel showered the rock walls and even splashed some men at the mouth of the cave directly above the trucks. Screaming men tumbled from the ledge, their clothes shrouded in crackling flames. Several more fortunate terrorists had been killed instantly in the blast.

The Chinook swerved away from the mountain and moved noisily over the treetops. The terrorists continued to fire after it. Manning returned fire with his assault rifle, killing some and driving others deeper back into the tunnels.

Encizo's MP-5 had less accuracy and range than a rifle. He crawled to the corpse of a slain terrorist farther back in the jungle and gathered up the dead man's AK-47. By quickly frisking the corpse, he also discovered two spare magazines. He turned to head back to the edge of the jungle to join Manning, but a slight movement by some trees near him caught his eye.

He swung the Kalashnikov toward the figure that staggered toward him, and immediately dropped it. Amir Said held an H&K subgun tucked under one arm as he dragged one leg, the other arm clutched to his side. Blood stained his shirtfront, and his trouser leg was soaked crimson below the knee. His face was damp and pale, and he breathed roughly and heavily, pink froth oozing from his lips.

"Get down, Amir!" Encizo yelled as he sprang toward him. "They might open fire any moment!"

Said dropped his weapon and sank against the trunk of an ironwood, sliding down to the base of the tree. Encizo saw a splinter of bone jutting from the split skin of his shin. The injured man looked up at him, his eyes filled with pain. He managed a weak smile.

"Mati..." Said began, and spit up blood. He realized he was speaking in his native language and switched to English. "Death...may not be so bad, but...but dying hurts like a bitch...."

He laughed at his own joke and coughed violently. Fresh globs of red spewed across his shirt. Encizo knelt beside his friend. He hardly noticed the blood that splashed him as he pushed Amir's arm aside to examine the wound. His stomach knotted. Said had two bullets in the chest. One had certainly hit a lung. The injury was obviously very serious.

"Be quiet and lie still," Encizo told him, and reached for the combat first-aid kit on his belt.

He lowered Said to the ground. The wounded man groaned and ground his teeth. Encizo removed some field dressing from his kit and tore open Said's shirt. The purple-and-red puckered flesh around the bullet holes leaked steady streams of blood. Encizo covered the wounds. He wished Calvin James was there, but he doubted that even the Phoenix medic could do anything to save Said.

"I...got one of them...before the machine guns...got me," Said told him with difficulty. His voice gurgled deep in his throat.

"Shut up," Encizo pleaded, and finished wrapping the wound as best he could. "The PMB is here. They'll have medics. They'll fly you to a hospital...."

"I'm not going...to make it," Said told him. "You know that... So do I."

Encizo was about to disagree, but he could not lie to Said. The guy deserved better than bullshit in the last moments of his life.

"Just lie still," he said gently, and placed a hand on Said's shoulder.

"We...we beat them...." Said declared. His ragged breath made it impossible for Encizo to tell if this was a statement or a question.

"We beat them," the Cuban agreed, and gently squeezed Said's shoulder. "I am so proud to have worked with you, Amir. We all feel that way...."

He felt Said's body tremble. The agent's eyes rolled back, and his mouth fell open. Encizo placed two fingers to the side of his neck in a vain effort to find a pulse. He closed his eyes and whispered a prayer he recalled from childhood. Then he raised his hand and crossed himself.

Before he turned away, the Cuban gently pushed Said's eyelids shut for the last time.

THE TERRORISTS might have begun to relax after the Chinook swerved away from their direct bombardment, but their relief was short-lived. Another gunship had suddenly appeared. A smaller, faster Huey Cobra swung down from the sky and sprayed the caves with machine gun fire. The terrorists were caught off guard. More bodies tumbled from the caves and slumped against the rock walls within.

The sleek dark helicopter whirled past the mountains and circled to make another pass. Flame spit from the barrel of the machine gun turret at its snout. It fired the first of several rockets mounted on both its sides. The missile sailed into a rock wall by the mouth of a cave. The explosion filled the cave with rubble and rock dust.

The chopper fired more and scored a couple of direct hits. The projectiles exploded inside the caves and blasted tons of debris—some of it human—from the openings. The Cobra swung around in another circle and began to make another pass.

While the Cobra continued its steady assault, the Chinook hovered above the trees, and PMB soldiers descended from the big helicopter to the jungle floor. With carabiners attached to harnesses, they slid rapidly down nylon ropes with gloved fists to the tree branches below. The soldiers shifted the lines past the branches and continued their descent to the ground.

Encizo recognized Major Tukarno as he and several other PMB troops approached on foot. They were heavily armed and carried canvas pouches with gas masks on their belts. Some soldiers carried grenade launchers, as well as submachine guns and assault rifles. Tukarno jogged up to Encizo. He stopped short and stared down at Amir Said's still body. Then he lowered his head solemnly. Whatever Said's religious beliefs might have been, the slain hero was honored by Tukarno's brief Muslim prayer, as well as Encizo's Catholic invocation.

"He was a good man," Encizo declared.

"Yes," said Tukarno. "I wish I had told him."

"There's always something you wish you'd said when it's too late to say it," the Cuban acknowledged quietly.

Police Mobile Brigade troops hurried on to the mountain. They fired tear gas grenades at the caves, pulling on their masks as they ran. Billows of green fumes drifted from the openings, but no more terrorists emerged to challenge the fresh troops. Apparently the fight had been taken out of them already—if any still survived.

"Sorry we didn't get here faster," Tukarno said as he and Encizo joined Gary Manning. "I managed to convince the base commander to assign the Bell gunship and arm it with rocket fire. It's a Cobra, an excellent name for a dangerous snake in the air."

"Yeah," Manning agreed. "The Cobra proved itself in Vietnam."

"The crew were trained by American Vietnam veterans," Tukarno added. "The commander assured me they were the best men for the job. I'm inclined to agree. The rest of us left in the Chinook while they saw to the Cobra. They took a while to join us, but that little gunship caught up pretty fast."

"That's the good news," Encizo told Manning. "The bad news is Amir's dead. The machine gun barrage chewed him up, and he died back there."

"I was afraid something had happened to him," the Canadian said, and shook his head sadly. "What about Colby and Collins?"

"I don't know," Encizo answered. "Maybe we should head around the other side of the mountain and see if they need any help."

"They're at the other side?" Tukarno asked with a frown. "I thought this mission was finished except for mopping up what's left in the caves."

"This mission won't be over until we can put a tombstone on the top of it," Manning replied as he shoved a fresh magazine into his G-3 rifle. "I just hope that we won't need any tombstones for Colby and Collins."

21

Rocks tumbled from the mountainside as Munap Djarios pushed the stones from the mouth of the tunnel. The big Indonesian completed his task and emerged from the tunnel, a Beretta M-12 submachine gun clenched in one large fist. He glanced about warily. The sounds of battle still raged in front of the mountain fortress, but he saw no one lurking by the two British Land Rovers or in the surrounding rain forest.

"*Datang,*" Munap said over his shoulder to the others in the tunnel.

Colonel Qui pushed his steamer trunk through the opening. Munap growled with annoyance at the additional luggage, but grabbed the handle at one end and hauled the trunk out. He wondered how long Qui had owned it. The Vietnamese insisted on dragging it everywhere he went. Munap knew that all Qui's worldly possessions were kept in it. Even so, the colonel had more than the Djarios brothers put together.

Qui climbed from the tunnel, a Tokarev outloader in his fist. The colonel was no longer dressed in his flowing robe, but was now in a khaki uniform and canvas boots. No rank or insignia was attached to the tunic, and he wore a conical hat instead of a service cap. Wordlessly he grabbed the handle at the other end of the trunk to help Munap carry it to the Land Rovers.

Hasan Djarios was the last man to climb from the tunnel. He wondered if Gunawan had seen them escape. The radioman had probably returned to the headquarters section to seek advice from his *Mérah Tentera* leaders. When he could not find them, he would know they had abandoned their comrades. Munap wondered whether or not Gunawan could find the secret tunnel that led to the other side of the mountain.

Leaving the others to face their fate alone disturbed the brothers. They had known many of their comrades for years. Some had been fellow inmates at Ek Penjara. They had loyally followed Hasan and Munap and they had trusted them implicitly.

Hasan knew he would never be free of the guilt of leaving them. He regretted that he had agreed to Qui's plan at the base in Bali, and he had sworn he would never again abandon his comrades. Yet when the time came to decide between standing with his fellow *Mérah Tentera* members in combat against forces that would almost certainly destroy them and saving his own life, Hasan had once again chosen the latter.

"Keep the headlights off," Qui told the brothers as they moved to the Land Rovers. "Don't turn them on, no matter how dark it may be. If we hit a tree or get caught in the mud, we'll simply have to walk to the river."

"The PMB may already have patrol boats looking for anyone who might get away," Munap warned.

"That's a chance we must take," the colonel insisted. "If we see the boats, we can hide in the forest."

They swung the trunk into the rear of a Rover. Hasan and Munap put their subguns in the back seat, and Qui climbed in beside them. The brothers took the front seat, Hasan behind the wheel. He turned the key in the ignition, but the engine would not turn over.

"What's wrong?" Qui demanded.

"It won't start," Hasan replied. "Isn't that obvious?"

He climbed from the vehicle and opened the hood. He found the problem immediately. The distributor cap had been removed, and the cords connecting the spark plugs had been pulled off. For good measure, the positive and negative cables from the battery had also been disconnected.

"You're not going anywhere this time," Yakov Katzenelenbogen announced as he stepped from the jungle with his MP-5 aimed at the Land Rover.

"Hands up, right now!" David McCarter added, and gestured with the barrel of his Heckler & Koch subgun.

Hasan slowly raised his hands. He thought of grabbing for his side arm, but realized he could not hope to draw it before the Phoenix pair would cut him down. Munap and Qui also thrust their hands overhead. The colonel stared at the prosthesis attached to Katz's abbreviated arm.

"Did you arrange this?" Qui inquired in English.

"Get out of the vehicle and make sure your friends understand," Katz replied in a hard voice. "If any of you reach for a weapon or even look suspicious, we'll open fire on all three of you."

Qui translated the message as he stepped from the Rover. Munap reluctantly followed his example. The big man carried the kris in his belt, but no pistol. The other two carried side arms, and Hasan's whip was also attached to his belt.

Katz and McCarter stood roughly three meters from their captives. The sounds of gunfire and explosions were subsiding on the opposite side of the mountain. Qui stepped forward. Katz aimed his MP-5 at the colonel's chest.

"Stay where you are," the Israeli warned.

"Of course," Qui assured him. "How did you guess we'd come out of a tunnel here?"

"You used the same tactic at the base in Bali," Katz answered. "It wasn't too hard to figure out. Especially when we found the Land Rovers."

"Maybe we should chat later," McCarter suggested. "Right now I reckon we should have these blokes lose their weapons."

"You heard the man," Katz told Qui. "One at a time. I wouldn't want you fellows to think we can be distracted by trying to watch you all at the same time. You go first, Colonel. Lower one hand, very slowly, and unbuckle your gunbelt. Let it drop and get the hand back up before we get nervous. Then tell your friend with the whip to do the same."

Qui obeyed instructions and carefully unbuckled the belt with one hand. It fell by his feet, and Qui kicked the rig toward Katz before he was told to do so. He told Hasan to follow his example. The Indonesian slowly lowered a hand to his belt, unbuckled it and allowed it to slip loose from his hip.

In a flash Hasan had snatched his *penjut* as the belt fell. He snapped the whip around Katz's wrist, the lash curling around the weapon like a killer python. Hasan yanked hard and pulled the gun from Katz's grasp.

Simultaneously McCarter swung his H&K chopper at the attacker and triggered a 3-round burst. Hasan's chest exploded in a spray of crimson. He toppled to the ground as Munap bellowed in rage. The big Indonesian pulled the kris from his belt and desperately threw the knife at the Briton before he even realized what he was doing.

"Bugger!" McCarter exclaimed as he raised his MP-5 to shield his chest.

The kris struck the subgun, the point snapping against the steel barrier. The blade broke and the knife fell harmlessly to the ground, but Munap had already charged forward. He swung a kick at McCarter's MP-5 and booted the weapon from the Briton's hands. Then he drove a powerful forearm into the commando's chest. McCarter reeled.

Katz reached for the Beretta pistol under his right armpit. Qui rushed forward as he pulled the weapon clear and soundly chopped the side of his hand across the Israeli's forearm near the wrist. The blow to the ulna nerve jarred the Beretta from Katz's hand. Qui instantly seized the Phoenix commander's arm at the wrist and elbow and turned sharply to haul Katz in an arm drag.

The Israeli was thrown into the side of the Land Rover, the hood slamming down from the impact. Qui pounced on Katz from behind and struck him between the shoulder blades. The Phoenix fighter fell hard against the Rover a second time, and Qui punched him in a kidney and hammered a fist into his upper back again. The Vietnamese heard the commando groan in pain as he started to slide along the vehicle. Then Qui whipped his garrote from one pocket and prepared to swing the loop over the dazed Israeli's head.

MUNAP'S FOREARM SMASH had knocked McCarter two meters backward, and the Briton barely managed to keep his balance as he gasped for the air that had been knocked out of him. Munap Djarios hit like a cricket bat, McCarter thought. He realized the big man was trained in some form of *pentjak-silat*, but he would not have known what *mustika kwitang* was. It would not have inspired him with any confidence to know that some practitioners of *mustika kwitang* demonstrate their ability by smashing coconuts with bare hands and forearm strokes.

Munap followed his brother's killer, his face twisted with raw fury. He swung a kick at the Briton's abdomen. McCarter blocked it with crossed forearms and hooked a kick of his own at Munap's side. The Phoenix commando's boot hit Munap under his rib cage. The Indonesian groaned and thrust a fist at his face. McCarter dodged and parried Munap's arm with a heel-of-the-palm stroke to the forearm. At the same time, McCarter drove his other fist into Munap's solar plexus.

McCarter swung a karate chop intended for the side of Munap's neck, but the big terrorist shifted a shoulder to block it. The Briton's hand bounced off thick muscle, and Munap whipped a back fist to the side of McCarter's face. It was a glancing blow, but hard enough to send him stumbling back again into the vegetation.

The big man charged forward. McCarter raised his arms to defend himself as Munap swung another forearm smash. The Briton was lifted off his feet and flung backward into a tree trunk. Pain shot through McCarter's spine as he hit the tree. Munap closed in and drove a fist into McCarter's abdomen. With his other hand he grabbed the side of McCarter's face and shoved his head into the trunk.

Munap prepared to smash his head into the tree once more as McCarter shifted his face slightly and clamped his teeth down as hard as he could on Munap's thumb. The terrorist cried out in pain and surprise.

The commando jabbed a fist to Munap's chin as he continued to bite the captive thumb. He grabbed his opponent's arms at the crooks of the elbows as he finally released the thumb and snapped his head forward to butt the front of his own skull into Munap's face. The Briton thought he heard his enemy moan, but the cry could have been his own. The tough Cockney had instinctively employed a favorite street-fighting tactic he had learned in the East End of London. He also made the painful discovery that head butting with a skull that had already been slammed into a tree trunk was particularly excruciating.

McCarter did not allow the pain to stop him, aware that he was fighting for his life. He followed the head butt with a solid punch and swung a boot toe into Munap's groin. The big man staggered backward and doubled up, blood oozing from his nostrils and mouth. The son of a bitch is human, after all, McCarter thought with some relief, and he hit Munap with a hard left hook for good measure.

Munap swayed and nearly fell. He swayed and quickly dropped to the ground to lash a leg at McCarter's ankles. The Briton had expected the maneuver, and he jumped nimbly over the "iron broom" leg sweep. Having missed his opponent, Munap quickly started to rise. McCarter kicked the Indonesian in the face before he could get up.

The terrorist fell on his back and kicked up from the ground. McCarter dodged again and grabbed Munap's leg. The grounded man shifted on the small of his back and lashed out with his other leg. The Briton's forearm struck Munap's calf muscle as he held on to the terrorist's other ankle with his left hand. McCarter secured the second leg and tucked the guy's shin under his arm. Then he stepped across his opponent and raised the trapped legs.

Munap was forced over on his belly by the pressure. McCarter held on to his opponent's legs and sat back on the terrorist. His spine bent at the unnatural angle by the Boston Crab hold, the big Indonesian struggled to try to break free, but McCarter held on and pulled back with all his might as his rump landed between Munap's shoulder blades. A crack at the small of Munap's spine announced that the lumbar vertebrae had finally snapped. Munap gasped and trembled slightly. McCarter felt the man's body go limp, and he released the legs of the corpse.

KATZ GLIMPSED the wire loop slipping over his face and he quickly thrust his hook under his chin. Qui pulled the garrote handles to tighten the noose, but the wire refused to close. The colonel grunted and pulled harder.

Instead Katz drove an elbow back into Qui's ribs. The Vietnamese gasped in surprise at the pain. The Phoenix commander rammed his elbow again and thrust his single left hand low to claw Qui's genitals. The Vietnamese moaned in agony and released the garrote. Katz let go his hold of the colonel's crotch and whirled to slash a back fist into his face.

Qui stumbled back a meter, confused and dazed. He stared at the garrote in the hooked grasp of Katz's artificial arm and suddenly realized what had happened. The Israeli dropped the garrote and approached his opponent, breathing heavily.

Qui attacked in desperation. He tried to throw a kick with his right foot and a punch with his left hand simultaneously. Katz met the kick with a boot to Qui's shin and deflected the punch with a sweep of his prosthesis. Then his fist slammed into Qui's jaw. The Asian's head recoiled from the blow, and Katz raised his hook.

The steel hooks clamped around the man's exposed throat and tightened, the metal points puncturing the soft flesh. With eyes bugging out, Qui flapped his arms in a hopeless effort to break free. Katz caught one arm with his left hand and tucked it under his armpit to hold him close and secure as the hooks tore out his throat. Blood spurted from Qui's severed arteries, and his struggles immediately ceased. The Phoenix Force commander dumped the corpse to the ground.

"I guess you don't need my help, after all," McCarter remarked as he approached his comrade, Browning pistol in his fist, barrel pointed at the sky.

Katz was panting. "I managed," he answered wearily as he stepped back from Colonel Qui's body. "Let's find out how the battle turned out around front."

"Looks like we won," McCarter announced with a grin, spying Manning and Encizo trotting their way along the dirt road.

CALVIN JAMES WALKED from the hospital with Major Tukarno by his side. The other members of Phoenix Force waited in a limousine van. They would be traveling to the airport in style. The black commando had benefited from his two days of rest in the hospital.

"You got to goof off for a while this time," Manning commented with a grin as he pushed open the van door for him.

"Yeah," James said with a weak smile. He climbed into the vehicle and took a seat with his teammates in the back. "I'm surprised you guys managed without me."

"Maybe if you'd been there, we could have saved Amir," Encizo said sadly.

"From the way you describe his injuries, I couldn't have done anything for him that you didn't do," James assured the Cuban. "You helped him through the last minutes. That's all anyone could have done."

"How are you feeling, Jones?" Katz inquired.

"Terrific," James answered. "Maybe I ought to get hit by shrapnel more often. It's about the only way I can get any rest in this job."

"We'd better head directly to the airport," Tukarno announced as he climbed in and closed the door. "That CIA agent Chappell has been badgering everyone from the

U.S. Embassy to the hospital staff to try to find out more details about you gentlemen. Probably best if you get out of the country before he convinces the local authorities to have you detained at the airport."

"Let him read the official version when it hits the newspapers," McCarter growled. "Dumb bastard probably won't even realize the story is connected with us."

"Some of us will know," Tukarno said fondly. "This has been the most extraordinary few days of my life. I'm glad it's over, but I regret you're leaving now. Perhaps sometime in the future, you'll return to Indonesia for a peaceful and more relaxed visit. If so, please contact me. Any or all of you are welcome in my home any time."

"Thank you, Major," Katz said with a nod. "We don't get much time off work, but if we ever get the chance, we surely will."

"Your superiors should be pleased with the news of the success of your mission," Tukarno remarked as the van pulled away from the curb and headed for the street.

"I'm sure they will be," Katz agreed. "Of course, they may have another one for us as soon as we arrive."

"Another mission?" Tukarno asked with a frown. "So soon?"

"There's always another mission," McCarter answered with a contented sigh. He would not have had it any other way.

DEATHLANDS®

A different world—a different war

RED EQUINOX $3.95 ☐
Ryan Cawdor and his band of postnuclear survivors enter a
malfunctioning gateway and are transported to Moscow, where
Americans are hated with an almost religious fervor and blamed
for the destruction of the world.

DECTRA CHAIN $3.95 ☐
A gateway that is part of a rambling underwater complex brings
Ryan Cawdor and the group off the coast of what was once
Maine, where they are confronted with mutant creatures and
primitive inhabitants.

ICE & FIRE $3.95 ☐
A startling discovery changes the lives of Ryan Cawdor and his
band of postholocaust survivors when they encounter several
cryogenically preserved bodies.

Total Amount	$ _____
Plus 75¢ Postage	_____ .75
Payment enclosed	$ _____

TAKE 'EM NOW

FOLDING SUNGLASSES
FROM GOLD EAGLE

Mean up your act with these tough, street-smart shades. Practical, too, because they fold 3 times into a handy, zip-up polyurethane pouch that fits neatly into your pocket. Rugged metal frame. Scratch-resistant acrylic lenses. Best of all, they can be yours for only $6.99.
MAIL YOUR ORDER TODAY.

Send your name, address, and zip code, along with a check or money order for just $6.99 + .75¢ for delivery (for a total of $7.74) payable to Gold Eagle Reader Service.
(New York residents please add applicable sales tax.)

Remove from pouch...

unfold once.

unfold twice..

and they're ready to wear.

GOLD EAGLE

Gold Eagle Reader Service
3010 Walden Avenue
P.O. Box 1396
Buffalo, N.Y. 14240-1396

GES-1AR

Offer not available in Canada.

Do you know a real hero?

At Gold Eagle Books we know that heroes are not just fictional. Everyday someone somewhere is performing a selfless task, risking his or her own life without expectation of reward.

Gold Eagle would like to recognize America's local heroes by publishing their stories. If you know a true to life hero (that person might even be you) we'd like to hear about him or her. In 150-200 words tell us about a heroic deed you witnessed or experienced. Once a month, we'll select a local hero and award him or her with national recognition by printing his or her story on the inside back cover of THE EXECUTIONER series, and the ABLE TEAM, PHOENIX FORCE and/or VIETNAM: GROUND ZERO series.

Send your name, address, zip or postal code, along with your story of 150-200 words (and a photograph of the hero if possible), and mail to:

LOCAL HEROES AWARD
Gold Eagle Books
225 Duncan Mill Road
Don Mills, Ontario
M3B 3K9
Canada